EARTHBOUND

CHILD OF GOD

EARTHBOUND
CHILD of GOD

by LAUREL PAYNE

**CREATION
HOUSE**

Earthbound Child of God by Laurel Payne
Published by Creation House
A Charisma Media Company
600 Rinehart Road
Lake Mary, Florida 32746
www.charismamedia.com

Unless otherwise noted, all Scripture quotations are from the Holy Bible, New International Version. Copyright © 1973, 1978, 1984, International Bible Society. Used by permission.

Scripture quotations marked NLT are from the Holy Bible, New Living Translation, copyright © 2007. Used by permission of Tyndale House Publishers, Inc., Wheaton, IL 60189. All rights reserved.

The names of persons mentioned or described in this book have been changed to preserve their privacy.

Front cover design assisted by artwork from Sue Brunner.

Design Director: Bill Johnson
Cover design by Nancy Panaccione

Visit the author's website: http://toyoufromgod.weebly.com/

Library of Congress Cataloging-in-Publication Data: 2011936190
International Standard Book Number: 978-1-61638-661-0
E-book ISBN: 978-1-61638-662-7

First edition

11 12 13 14 15 — 987654321
Printed in Canada

Contents

PREFACE

Dear Reader,

Earthbound Child of God is about a teenage girl's dreams, longings, struggles, and accomplishments. However, some parts of this story describe my personal struggles, longings, and dreams. You and I may be different in many ways, but in other ways we are very much the same. Samantha's journey in life tells the story of your life, as it tells the story of mine in some ways. Each of our struggles, dreams, longings, accomplishments, etc., may not be as intense, severe, or happy as others, but we all have experienced some form of neglect, harm, or happiness. We are not alone. God will be there for you like He has been there for me. God saved my life and the words *thank you* never seem to be enough. He knows my heart and will guide me down the road of eternity. I pray that you will allow or continue to allow Him to walk with you, or at times, carry you. Let God be that shoulder to cry on, that missing father or mother in your life, that crutch to lean on, or whatever analogy you need Him to be in your life; let Him be that, as He was and still is for me. God has become the Father I have always wanted in my life, full of love and compassion. I was a depressed and lost teenager desperate and confused about how to be loved for who I was. When I hit rock bottom, God held out His hand and pulled me from the deep, dark hole I was in. His love, grace, and compassion, along with many other characteristics, have changed my life. Let Him change or continue to change your life. He loves you unconditionally, as I also love you...always.

Sincerely with love,

Laurel Payne

> But those who trust in the lord will renew their strength. They will soar high on wings like eagles. They will run and not grow weary. They will walk and not faint.
> —ISAIAH 40:31, NLT

PROLOGUE

June 17, 2018 at 3:18 a.m.

Dear Diary,

Tonight I'm planning on grabbing the little backpack I keep under the floorboard in my closet that has a photo of me and Momma, the photos of myself, the videos I secretly started recording around age ten, that video of my sixth birthday I stole from dad in the cellar, and Meeko, my raccoon rag doll Mother made for me when I was three years old; and getting out of this awful place once and for all. It's not like I'll be missed or anything. I mean, my only purpose here is like Cinderella serving her evil stepmother and stepsisters; only I serve a sickening, disgusting so-called father. I don't think I can live in agonizing pain that keeps me up at night anymore. The whole idea of right now and every night and day wondering if he will come into my room and throw me around like a worthless rag doll or take away my innocence for no reason just terrifies me.

I wish Mom were here, even though she's out in the backyard under the cherry tree. I miss her warm, comforting bear hugs, the softness of her voice, the way she smiled and laughed, the times we would spend together cooking or baking, and how she would talk about my grandmother, who was Cherokee Indian, and my grandfather, who was White. A big part of my security blanket is gone and I'm left here scared and completely alone, except for Yeller, my best friend, who looks like a yellow lab mutt. I found him wandering around one of the rodeos two years ago. He knows to stay away from here, but when I leave the house I bring some leftovers for him, and he meets me by the park two blocks away to walk me to school or work. He goes with me everywhere.

It doesn't take a genius to know that if I stay here it won't be long 'til I'm going to be buried right beside my mother under the cherry tree. I'm tired of having to sneak out of the house to go to school, work, or a horse competition. I can't hang out with friends for fear of getting caught. I hear friends talk about my house (they don't know it's my house), saying that the man who lives there will take any kid who sets foot on the grounds inside the house, and that kid is never heard from again. There are rumors that he first tortures them, then buries them alive—which technically isn't far from the truth if you think about it. I mean, if I didn't live here and passed this house, and saw the six-foot fence with the pointed spikes and rolls of bob wire across the top (which is a pain to climb), the two male pit bulls that charge and snarl at any sound of movement, not to mention the long, eerie dirt road that goes deep into the darkness of trees that leads back towards the house, I might think the same thing.

My friend, Dustin, whom I met a few years ago, has talked to his parents and they have agreed to let me live with them on their ranch. I'm so excited! I can start living a life without so much worry; but it will take a while to get used to, I will admit. I will be able to pursue my riding career and schooling without having to do it in secret. Sure, I'll still have to be on my guard in case my father decides to hunt me down with those three friends of his.

Well, I better get going and get breakfast ready before my father gets up and his friends get here.

Samantha Bennett

Chapter One

THE HORROR

For he will command his angels concerning you to guard you in all your ways; they will lift you up in their hands, so that you will not strike your foot against a stone.

—PSALM 91:11–12

IT HAD BEEN three hours since Dustin and I left for the Texas Lone-Star Rodeo. As we arrived at the rodeo grounds I sensed something was wrong, but I couldn't figure out what. We took my horse, Guardian, to his living quarters to await tomorrow's big day.

"What a day, huh, Dustin?"

"No kiddin' Sam, I'm exhausted."

He plopped onto the bed and pulled his favorite worn black cowboy hat over his face, and groaned.

"Aw! You poor thing, do you need a nap?" I teased.

Dustin lifted his battered black hat revealing his dark chocolate-brown eyes, glinting at me with his soft-kissing lips crawling up the left side of his face. I could see the young nineteen-year-old teenager trying not to crack a smile, but he was unable to hide the boyish face I had fallen in love with.

"What did you say, baby?"

"You heard me." I couldn't help myself from giggling.

"All right, Samantha, you asked for it!"

With that he sat up, grabbed one of the big white bed pillows, and threw it at me, hitting me square in the face.

"Ah! You little...!" I picked up the pillow and threw it back at him with all I had. This went on for a little over an hour.

Later we headed out to Dustin's black Dodge 3500 Dooly and drove downtown to grab a bite at an Italian restaurant with some friends. Soon after we arrived, our rodeo pals drove up in Adam's red Ford F-150. It looked like Layn and Adam were cracking up at one of Skyler's hilarious jokes. We all said our hellos and went inside to eat. Dustin talked to Skyler and Layn about his new rifle; don't ask, I don't know what kind of rifle. Adam talked to me about what he'd been up to at his ranch, and I told him what I'd been up to as well. The waitress came and went with our food and drinks. Before long, all of us were done and ready to head back to hit the sack. The boys said their goodbyes and drove off. Dustin and I walked back to the truck and headed back to the hotel.

"Nice dinner, huh, Dustin?"

"Yeah, sure was. Man, you can never get tired of Skyler's jokes no matter how many times you have heard them."

"That is very true. Well, good night Dustin, love you."

"Good night Sam, love you."

Soon after falling asleep I began to dream....

> "What do you mean you're part Cherokee?
> This is outrageous!"
>
> "Now Charles, calm down. Let's not ruin
> Samantha's family birthday party."
>
> "Don't you dare tell me what to do, missy!
> You know, my father was right about you and
> I didn't listen to him. This has gone too far,
> Lillian!"
>
> Bang!
>
> "Mama!"

I awoke with a scream, accidentally waking up Dustin, and crying like the world was coming to an end. Dustin got off his bed and came over and wrapped his arms around me.

"You're OK, baby. You're safe now, shh."

He held me, rocking me back and forth as I cried and wailed into his warm chest, breathing in the faint sent of his cologne with every breath I took, until I fell back to sleep.

February 4, 2023 at 1:20 p.m.

Dear Diary,

Sorry for waiting five years to write to you. I've just lost track of time enjoying myself and my new life with Dustin and his family, and the new friends I've made. I'm so happy! Yeller and I are right at home. Dustin and I have moved our friendship up to the next level, and we have been dating now for a year. Being with him makes that "hole" in my heart fill up with such happiness it makes my insides want to explode. He is such a sweet, respectful, and loving gentleman. I love how I can talk to him about anything and know with such certainty that he will listen to me and be concerned for me—it's comforting. He and his parents know my situation, about my father, so they all try to support me and care for me the best way they know how, which is more than I could ever ask for. I love them all so much, especially Dustin. I hope someday Dustin will ask me to marry him.

Being able to see the boys again was so much fun. It was another stroll down memory lane; sitting at the table hearing all the jokes, the laughs seeping through the cracks, our mouths eating up every little detail of our lives, and with smiles of joy on all our faces.

It's amazing how quickly a fun night ending with a good night's sleep can turn into a sleepless night. It's interesting how just a dream can affect the rest of your night, the following day, then eventually your everyday life. The feeling of being watched, followed, or chased lingers in the back of your mind, keeping you on your guard; not wanting to say much out of fear of what will happen if you do; wondering if with every touch comes a visible or not-so-visible price. These and many other thoughts haunt me after so many sleepless nights. . .when will I not have to live every waking day like this? I want to live a life where I don't have to continuously look over my shoulder, jump or flinch with every touch, and can be able to join a conversation with ease.

Sincerely,

Samantha Bennett

Chapter Two

8 SECONDS...

Be merciful to me, O God, for men hotly pursue me; all day long they press their attack. My slanderers pursue me all day long; many are attacking me in their pride. When I am afraid, I will trust in you. In God, whose word I praise, in God I trust; I will not be afraid.

—PSALM 56:1–4

EVERY RODEO IS always the same—the crowds woopin' and a-hollerin', the smell of fresh-popped popcorn filling the stands, mixed with the smells of the livestock; bulls screaming, horses nickering; and if that's not enough, your friends yelling, "Where's this? Where's that? Dude, you're next—hurry up!" That's how rodeos are supposed to be, right?

"Sam, Guardian has to beat Glow N Ember's time for barrels otherwise you won't get into the finals."

"I know, Dustin, I know. Don't worry. I have faith in him and that's all we need."

"Next up, Samantha Bennett and Answered Prayers!"

As my name blared over the intercom I couldn't help but feeling like someone was watching me; but whom?

Guardian bolted out of the gate, swift and steady as ever, going around each barrel as if he knew where and when to place his feet. We elegantly glided around the third and final barrel like we were floating on air; this quickly switched into an angry mob charge as we were clear to run back through the gate with no time to spare. But as we were charging through, out of the blue, a raging bull gouged through the exit and came straight towards us! I sat deep in the saddle; Guardian skidded to a stop and quickly spun in the other direction. With no time to waste, I thought of a plan.

"Dustin! Throw me a rope!"

Dustin tossed the rope just as I brushed by him, with only a second to react. I spun Guardian to face the raging bull, still chasing us with all content.

My heart was pounding, but my mind was racing. Guardian started to back up quickly, but kept his eye on the bull. I began to twirl the rope around my head.

I counted in my head, "One, two, three, now!"

Guardian reared, then lunged toward the bull. The bull stopped for a second or two, thinking about what had just happened. His eyes gleamed with satisfaction, and he began to charge again. My plan was working so far, but how far would it go? Almost head to head with the beast, I threw the rope around the bull's throat, while Guardian cut a hard left, and I jumped out of the saddle right towards the bull. I landed on the ground, planting my feet full force, and tugged down farther and farther. I tried to bend his head sideways and down, avoiding the horns, so I could look into his eyes. All I saw was hatred and confusion; it wasn't necessarily toward me, but toward whom, I don't know. Nevertheless he was trying to run me over with loads of determination. I had no choice, but to go to plan "B."

I lunged myself outward and thrust myself onto the bull's back. The crowd gasped, surprised by the action I had taken. It's a good thing I'd snuck a few rides on the bulls back home. The bull was jumping this way and that, springing in circles so tight I could have sworn he was even making the audience sick to their stomachs.

Hoping this plan would work, I grabbed for the rope, still wrapped around his neck, lunged myself onto the ground, faced him, and, as I was heading to the ground, I gave him a good hard tug sideways and down. This caused him to kneel down and hit the ground with a "*thug!*" I stood up, breathing heavily. Guardian trotted up to me, and I mounted him, and at that moment the crowd cheered! I tugged on the rope to get the bull up and all three of us left the ring with the crowd woopin' and hollerin' in the background. Dustin ran right over to me before I could let my feet touch the ground.

"Oh my gosh! Baby, are you OK? That was some pretty daring stuff you did."

"Yeah, Dustin I'm alright. I just wish I knew how and why?" Just as those words left my mouth Adam saw something quite interesting.

"Hey Sam you might want to have a look at this."

I came around the bull and looked at his left flank.

"Oh my gosh! It looks like someone came from behind and thrashed him with a whip or something." Gashes of skin and blood were oozing from the wound.

By this time, Dustin had come around to see what was so interesting.

"Yep, it sure does, Sam. But the question is, how did it get there?"

"I don't know Dustin, I don't know."

February 6, 2023 at 4:22 p.m.

Dear Diary,

The strangest things happened this weekend. A bull came charging into the arena during my barrel racing. It seemed, since the bull had whiplash-type markings on his rear, that someone had opened the bull's pen, then lashed at him so he would charge out and into the arena. Weird, and yet I think I know who might have done it. Give you one guess.... Yep, my father. My question is, how did he know I was there? I have no idea and I prefer not to know. But now Dustin and I have about two and a half hours of driving left and I'm pretty tired, so I'm going to take a nap. I'll try to write more often.

Samantha Bennett

Chapter 3

FRESH START OF AN
OLD BEGINNING

...A cord of three strands is not quickly broken.
—ECCLESIASTES 4:12

DUSTIN, SKYLER, LAYN, Adam and I strolled down the midway decked out in our western show outfits, laughing and enjoying life like tomorrow was forever away. The sound of kids screaming ringing in our ears, the smells of funnel cakes and corn dogs making our mouths water, and the faint sound of some country artist singing over the loudspeakers always seemed to bring me back to a time full of simple pleasures.

Skyler and Layn went to get some corn dogs and sodas for Dustin, Adam, and me while we got some tickets for a few rides before our music gig at seven o'clock.

"Hey, when Skyler and Layn come back let's head over to the Ferris wheel before we have to start setting up for tonight," I offered openly.

"I'm actually going to go look at the gun booth we passed down yonder, but I'm sure Layn or Skyler wouldn't mind either—or they might just go and try to pick up some girls or something," Adam responded.

We waited for Skyler and Layn over by the fun house. Layn needed to find some new gun shells for his rifle, so he decided to go with Adam to the gun booth. Surprisingly, though, Skyler for once didn't want to go off and chase girls. This, quite honestly, was kind of odd. So, the three of us rode the Ferris wheel and were planning on meeting Adam and Layn by the barn entrance where we were to perform. Dustin and I sat next to each other while Skyler sat across in awkward silence. Looking down on the fair from so high up, seeing specks of children running around and the lights shining below, showed a whole new perspective on our world below. During the whole ride, however, Skyler kept staring at me. I tried to ask him what he was staring at and what was wrong, but when I did he would only snap out of his trance and say, "Oh, sorry, nothing."

Dustin kept glancing at Skyler, cocking his head to the side and looking at him with deep concern.

The Ferris wheel came around and stopped at the exit. Skyler jumped up from his seat and rushed out, speed walking in the direction of the barn where we would be performing. Dustin and I glanced at one another wondering what his problem was before we walked off the Ferris wheel and headed over to the barn, wrapped in each other's arms.

As we walked through the barn doors the atmosphere was full of life, with woopin' and a-hollerin', people trying to sing along, and the beat of boots brought into the music as they danced around the dance floor. Dustin walked towards the dance floor and stopped to face me, his hand held out.

"I believe we have time for one dance before we go on stage. May I have this dance, Miss Samantha Bennett?"

A big smile crept up my face as I blushed before replying...

"Of course, Mr. Dustin Samuel James."

Across the dance floor we glided and spun with grace and precision. I could faintly hear "Would You Go With Me" by Josh Turner in the background, as this world slowly drifted away, bringing us back in time to when we first met here at this very rodeo ten years ago.

I was eight years old and he was ten at the time.

I had about a two-hour break before I had a barrels competition for a client, so I decided to walk
around the horse barn. When I headed towards the
back stalls, I noticed a group of four boys around
my age sitting on top of hay bales that were leaning
up against the wall. One of the boys, who seemed
to be telling a joke, had sandy blonde hair with
grayish-green eyes and wore a straw cowboy hat,
and was dressed in a crazy red button-down shirt,
blue jeans and bright red cowboy boots. Two of the
boys were laughing at his joke. One had red hair
with ocean-blue eyes and was wearing a tan cowboy
hat, green button-down shirt, jeans, and light brown
cowboy boots. The other boy had light brown hair
with hazel eyes, a dark brown cowboy hat, and
a white plaid button-down shirt, jeans, and dark
brown cowboy boots. The last boy, who was staring
at me, had dark brown hair, dark brown eyes that
kind of reminded me of a Hershey's chocolate bar,
and a dark blue button-down shirt with a matching
black cowboy hat and boots.

The other three boys turned their heads to see
what the boy in the dark blue shirt was staring at.
The boy who had previously told the joke began
to laugh; however, the others looked at him, surprised—then at the boy in the blue shirt—then back
at me. I felt my cheeks turn red with embarrassment. The boy in the blue shirt took his gaze off me
and turned towards boy that was laughing at me.

"Hey, Skyler, shut it!"

He jumped down from the hay bales and started
to walk over to me, while two of the boys followed

him. The boy named Skyler sat on the hay bales stunned for a second before coming over.

"Hi, my name is Dustin, and this is Adam, and this is Layn."

Adam was the boy in the white button-down outfit and Layn was the boy in the green button-down outfit.

"Hi, I'm Samantha, or sometimes Sam."

"So, what event are you doing?" Dustin asked.

"Oh, I'm doing barrels today. How about you?"

"Team ropin', we all do it."

"Cool."

"Yeah. Say, later, after the events, would you like to go ride some rides with us?"

"Oh, I'm...yeah, OK."

"Great, see ya later."

With that they left to go get ready for their event. We have been best friends ever since. Even though we don't live in the same town, we all get together at the rodeos and continue where we left off.

February 7, 2023 at 12:13 a.m.

Dear Diary,

Being able to spend time with the boys tonight was very enjoyable. Watching Layn try to walk through the bubble house was hilarious! I think he will be hiccupping up bubbles for a few weeks. The face he made after he slipped into that massive clump of bubbles was totally priceless! But, when Adam and Layn went to look at gun shells and Skyler decided to stay with Dustin and me, I thought that was very strange and kind of awkward. I wonder what his deal is. And the way he kept staring at me was very scary and creepy. Dustin and I didn't like it one bit. Dustin wanted to talk to him when we got off the Ferris wheel, but Skyler bolted off to the barn before he had the chance to. Later that night I saw a glimpse of Skyler leaving the barn. He's been acting very strangely lately, especially around me...almost like he likes me or something. Guess I'll have to talk to him and clear the air, because I don't like him in that way at all—besides, he's a little too immature for me. Well I'm going to go to bed; last day of competition starts tomorrow at 11:00 a.m.

Samantha Bennett

Chapter 4

ENCORE RE-RUN

It is unthinkable that God would do wrong, that the Almighty would pervert justice.

—JOB 34:12

*R*ING-RING!
   "Hello?"
   "Hey Sam, it's Lilly. You want to go see *Backstage Pass* with Molly, Heather, and me at nine thirty tonight at the Addison Theater?"
   "Yeah, I'd love to!"
   "Great! We'll pick you up around eight o'clock so we can grab a bite to eat before the movie, OK?"
   "Sounds good, see you then."
   I hung up the phone just as Dustin came through the screen door.
   "Who was that?" Dustin asked.
   "Oh, that was Lilly. We are going to see *Backstage Pass* at nine thirty at the Addison Theater with Molly and Heather. They are picking me up at eight so we can go eat beforehand."
   "Oh, OK, that's great that you are having a girls' night out. Maybe I'll see if Adam, Skyler, and Layn want to do something."
   "Yeah, that would be a good idea! You can have a boys' night and I'll have a girls' night."
   Dustin came up and wrapped his arms around me and whispered, "Just as long as you will be safe" into my ear.
   I smiled and shrugged my shoulders as a chill went down my spine. I turned around wrapping my arm around his waist, and looked deep into his eyes as I said, "Of course."
   The tension in his back relaxed as he sighed a soft, reassuring sigh. The day came and went and before we knew it we were cuddled together on the couch drinking some homemade warm apple cider Dustin's mother had made.

Beep-beep!

"That's Lilly, I'd better get going."

"No you don't...stay here with me."

Dustin held onto me as if I was his long lost toy he had miraculously found. I giggled then turned around and gave Dustin a deep, sincere kiss on the lips. The horn echoed again from outside.

"I really have to go, babe. Girls' night out, remember?"

"Yeah, yeah, I remember." Dustin let me go, and as I walked out the front door he yelled,

"Love you, babe!"

With that he blew me a kiss for me to catch. I mouthed the words, "I love you" and blew him a kiss right back as I shut the door behind me.

I climbed into Lilly's blue Ford Focus with Heather and Molly in the back seat and we were off into town. We stopped and ate at the Mexican restaurant on Southwest 16th Street before seeing *Backstage Pass.*

The theater was on Addison Avenue in the downtown area of our hometown, Louisville, Kentucky. The old Victorian buildings lining the streets, music streaming out of the restaurants and bars, and lights lighting up the sky in the night brought you back to another time. The theater itself took you further back in time then you could ever imagine. An awning branched out towards the street and rows of lights shined below it. The doors were made of glass with an accent of shiny brass around the doors and door handles; billboard-type signs advertised what was playing each night in big, bold, black letters as lights traveled around them. The people working behind the ticket booths wore black dress shoes with black slacks, white button-up shirts with either a black tie or bow, and red jackets. We waited in line to get the tickets, then headed into the theater.

"We are sitting in row K seats 212, 213, 214, and 215," Lilly confirmed.

We all sat in our seats and enjoyed the show until intermission. Lilly and Molly went to the concessions area to get something to drink while Heather and I walked around the lobby to stretch our legs.

"So, how are you and Dustin, Samantha?" Heather asked.

"We are fine, thanks. How are you? Is there anything or anybody new in your life?"

"I'm pretty good and nothing new, really, aside from adopting Duke the basset hound from the animal shelter a few weeks ago."

"Aw, how is Duke doing? Adjusting well with Rascal the mutt?"

"Yeah, ha-ha, pretty well thanks."

Lights flickered above us as we continued walking down the hallway.

"Oh, we'd better head back to our seats, the show's about to start again," Heather noted.

When we returned, Lilly and Molly were already in their seats waiting for us. The second half of the show ended after about an hour. The crowd stood and applauded as the actors and actresses came out from behind the curtain, then began to leave just as the curtains closed for the last time until the next show. We filed out and into the crowd.

As Lilly, Heather, and Molly went through the double doors into the lobby, I got stuck behind a slow elderly couple and eventually lost sight of them.

I tried to call for them, but none of them could hear me with all the commotion. I moved to the side so I could look through my purse to find my cell phone so I could call Lilly to tell her to wait for me. As I was looking through my purse, someone came up behind me and whispered, "*Keep moving.*"

My body froze and my eyes widened, but I did as the voice said. Fear overcame my body and I was trying to think of a way out, wishing that someone would notice that something was wrong. I walked through the crowd, pushing through them as I went, thinking that I could lose the man behind me if I hurried through the array of people. But the man stayed right on top of my heels. I went through the front doors scanning for Lilly, Heather, or Molly, but the people from the show kept clustering too close together for me to see them anywhere.

"Go right," the manly voice whispered in a stern, husky voice.

I turned right heading towards the corner of Patterson Avenue and Addison Avenue. As I started walking closer to Patterson Avenue, three other men came from the shadows and followed us. There was one man on either side of me, and I heard the other one start walking behind me. They herded me down Patterson Avenue and further down I could see an abandoned-looking van. My insides began to panic.

As I was secretly trying to find a way out, I found a little alleyway on the other side of the street up ahead. It was my only chance of escape, so I took it. I ran as fast as I could towards the alleyway, but no matter how fast I ran it seemed to be getting further and further away. The three men lunged and wrestled me to the ground as "the leader" came from behind me, wrapped his arm around my neck, and pulled me to the ground. I tried to escape their grasps, but with every thrash and scream came punches and kicks to every part of my body. I tried to scream, but no words could escape my mouth. At some point during all the commotion "the leader" had left, but only to return with something dangling in his hand that I saw from the corner of my eye.

"Shut up, you worthless brat!" "the leader" yelled at me.

Before I could exchange two words in reply to his comment, everything went dark. When I woke, my ears were ringing and my head hurt. I tried to get my bearings and figure out where I was. I looked around and saw a variety of hunting trophies and a case of rifles. I seemed to have been placed against one of the walls on a bearskin rug next to the fireplace. As my eyes adjusted to the light, I saw the four men knelt beside me, staring at me, smiling. I stiffened and tried to back away.

My eyes landed on the man in the middle. He had dark, greasy brown hair, menacing green eyes, and a suit that he must have worn to the theater. His hand reached out towards my face. I tried to scoot away but I couldn't get much further than the wall I was propped against. His hand ran through my hair and down my face. My whole body trembled with fear, but I tried to keep my cool.

"Shh, Daddy's here."

My face hardened and my back stiffened. I looked

straight into his dark eyes and yelled in his face, "You are no father of mine!"I spat in his face then dove to the floor towards the door. His face turned red with rage as he screamed, "Get her before she escapes, and bring her back to 'the room'!"

The three men scrambled to their feet and ran after me. I was just reaching for the door handle when someone from behind me grabbed my feet and took them out from under me. I fell to the floor face-first. The man twisted my foot around and I flipped over onto my back. I tried to get away from his grasp, but one man came up and grabbed my arms while the other took my other foot. I thrashed my whole body trying to get away as they carried me away from the door, but I was unsuccessful. They brought me into a room and threw me onto an old worn spring mattress, and tied my hands and feet to the metal bedposts. My father leaned over me, his left hand by my shoulder, and whispered into my ear...

"Let's see how you get out of this one."

His lips delicately rested on my neck as he raised his face away from my ear to look into my eyes. He got off the bed without saying a word, then motioned for the three men to follow him out of the room. He let the men go out first and shut the door behind him as he blew me a sickening kiss.

The ropes began rubbing into my flesh, causing a burning sensation that shot through my arms and legs. I lay there on the bed staring at the ceiling as the springs from the mattress pressed into my back. After what felt like hours, I heard the door creak open. I raised my head to see who had come through the door, hoping it was Dustin or someone coming to my rescue, but to my disappointment it was just one of the men from my father's "posse." He had long, rough, dirty brown hair, pale blue eyes, a worn white undershirt with a blue plaid button-up shirt covered in dirt and stains, and blue jeans that practically would be considered shredded with all their holes and stains. I heard the sound of his large heavy boots as he came up next to the bed and sat right by me, just looking at me.

"What?" I asked in a hoarse, defensive tone.

"Nothing," he replied, but the way he answered and kept looking at me made me believe that whatever he was thinking was more than just nothing.

An awkward silence filled the room. I began to feel uneasy with him just silently sitting at my bedside, gazing into my face. I tried to move somewhat away from him, but the minute I started to move he placed his hand on my lower stomach very lightly, as if he was telling me not to move, without words. I froze and fear swelled up in my body; I didn't know what to do or what was going to happen.

"Shh...there's no need to be afraid," he reassured me quietly.

He then leaned in towards me, his hand moving slowly further down my stomach. I tried to sink into the mattress but I could only go so far before the springs dug into my back. Tears rolled down my face as his lips touched mine. The taste of tobacco filled my mouth, making me want to puke. Eventually his lips released mine; he got off the bed, then walked out the door, shutting it behind him.

Silent tears rolled down my face. I tried not to get

hysterical, for I was afraid my father or someone else would come back into the room. I longed for someone to come to my rescue and save me from this reality I had been trying to escape. No matter how hard I tried, it always came back into my life to haunt me.

Hours continued to pass late into the night and into the early morning. The sounds of the wilderness came to life as I heard the crickets chirping, the frogs croaking and eventually the sound of birds singing. I must have fallen asleep sometime late in the night, for very early in the morning I woke with a start to a scratching sound coming from outside. I looked towards the window and there was Yeller, my bud of a mutt, peering into the window. Tears of joy and comfort went down my face. Yeller left the window and I heard him outside sniffing his way around, trying to find a way inside. I could hear him pacing back and forth behind me for sometime, then he stopped and it sounded like he started digging or scratching again at the wall behind me. A few minutes later I heard footsteps from outside behind me. I feared that one of the men or my father might have heard Yeller outside, until I heard a voice whisper, "Good boy."

I heard something that sounded like an axe going up against the wood. A few minutes later Yeller jumped on the bed and began gnawing on the ropes. I couldn't believe it; I was so overcome with relief that someone had come to my rescue. But I wondered who was outside. I kept checking the door hoping that no one would come through while Yeller was in the room; thankfully, by the time Yeller had me untied, there was no sign of movement on the other side of the door.

I attempted to turn over onto my stomach, but the pain was too great and my body was too stiff from lying on my back for hours on end to move. Yeller gently stepped over me, went to my other side, and rolled me over. I held my tongue as he did so, so I wouldn't wake my father and the three men, in case they were on the other side of the door. I lay on my stomach unable to move, but no worries—Yeller cautiously grabbed my arm and slowly began to pull me off the bed, onto the floor and out a hole that wasn't there before. The minute Yeller and I were both outside, I was rolled over onto my back. I vaguely saw a young man over me and he knelt down to lift me up into his arm. Before I could utter the word...*Dustin*...I passed out.

When I came around and got a hold of my surroundings, I realized I was in another room lying in another bed. I started to panic and screamed. The door ahead of me burst open and Dustin ran across the room and wrapped his arm around me.

"Shh...Sam, shh...you're OK, shh."

I was hysterical, and I cried and shook uncontrollably in his arms. I intertwined with his arms and buried myself in his body, not wanting to let go. We both held onto one another, crying and rocking back and forth together. At some point during our sobs and hiccups, Yeller jumped onto the bed and came in between Dustin and me, almost pushing Dustin off the bed, and started licking my face. I fell back onto the pillows and started laughing.

"Yeller, quit it...ha-ha...quit!"

Dustin sat stunned at what just happened, then he too started laughing and joined in the fun.

July 2, 2023 at 9:10 p.m.

Dear Diary,

Last night was pretty interesting if I do say so myself. I really enjoyed going out with the girls to the theater. It was nice to go out and have girl time. Don't get me wrong, hanging with the boys is very fun too, but sometimes a woman needs some time either to herself or with other women. I really had fun dressing up for an occasion other than going on a date.

Backstage Pass was a romance about a young girl who tries to pursue a job in acting on Broadway. Along the way she meets this boy and together they find out more about themselves and what they really want out of life. It was like they were destined for one another, to pursue something far greater than acting on Broadway. It really reminded me of Dustin and myself, just under different circumstances. So, about halfway through the show I really began to miss him...especially since my father apparently had been hanging out in the crowd that night, and later he ambushed me. I really wished Dustin had been there with me to protect me.

When I was lying on that bed tied up, I was terrified that it was the end, or that something far worse was going to happen. The man—I think his name is Joe—is the quietest one out of the group. It seems to me that somewhere inside of him he has more of a purposeful morality. I'm not sure, but it seems like he knows that what he and the others are doing is wrong, but he just goes along with it out of terror of my father, "the boss." I wouldn't really blame him; my father is a terrible, scary man.

I have to say, though, I sure was relieved and happy to see Yeller looking at me through the window! He is my hero! I don't know what I would do without him—or Dustin, or Guardian for that matter.... Well I'm going to go. Talk to you soon.

Samantha Bennett

Chapter 5

A SUMMER BREEZE
FULL OF WONDER

And in him you too are being built together to become a dwelling in which God lives by his Spirit.

—EPHESIANS 2:22

S ITTING ON TOP of Heaven's Peak looking into the distance of the sunset sky, the faint sound of the wind whispering into my ear as it brushes through my hair and against my face, brings me back to a time when I had no worries or concerns and my life was free.

It was a midsummer afternoon with the sun out, horses whinnying and nickering in the distance, and the wind rustling in the trees. Dustin and I were sitting on the porch swing wrapped in each other's arms. We heard the sound of boots and spurs as the screen door swung open. Dustin and I looked up just as Dustin's dad turned to face us, resting against the porch railing.

"Hey, why don't we all go up to Cumberland Falls and stay in a log cabin this year for our family vacation?" Dustin's father asked us.

Dustin and I looked at one another, then both replied, "Sounds good to us."

"Good, now we just have to check with your mother."

"Dad, Mom will be fine with it. She loves anything to do with the outdoors; not sure how she'll react to the whole camping thing, though."

"Thanks, Dustin, that's reassuring," he replied with a sarcastic tone, then smiled as he turned to go back into the house.

Three weeks later Mr. and Mrs. James, Dustin, and I packed our bags and headed out on the long drive to Cumberland Falls, Kentucky. We pulled up to the cabin in Mr. James's black Ford Super Duty. The men unloaded the truck, while Mrs. James and I got the cabin homey and ready for the joy and blessings of tomorrow and the rest of the vacation days to come. The first few days out at Cumberland Falls we went on nature walks, hiking and mountain biking adventures, and had a few picnic lunches. Friday evening, Mr. James decided to take Mrs. James out for a night on the town. He offered for Dustin and me to join them since he didn't want to leave us at the cabin by ourselves. We agreed, but, with one exception: a portion of the evening had to be a "romantic" escape for just the two of them, and for us. He was OK with the idea, although he was not quite comfortable leaving just the two of us alone to roam around the town; but, it was better than leaving us here at the cabin alone. Dustin and I knew he wasn't exactly comfortable about it, but we felt like he and Mrs. James deserved to have some time alone together on this vacation.

All four of us drove into town. Dustin was dressed in a green plaid button shirt and black denim jeans, with his black boots and cowboy hat; Mr. James was dressed in a crisp, white button-down shirt with black boots and jeans; Mrs. James wore a golden yellow dress with a hint of green, and brown heels; and I wore a sunset-orange-colored dress with brown designs along the bottom, with brown flats.

Dustin and I left his parents as they walked into what looked like a semiformal restaurant. We continued down the sidewalk, debating where we should eat, and decided on a little hamburger joint. We enjoyed two hamburgers and two milkshakes, and split a side order of fries outside under the starry night sky. When we finished our hamburgers,

Dustin and I strolled down the sidewalk towards the outskirts of the town until we came across a small abandoned park that was lit up by the mysterious full moon and bright stars. Dustin took my hand and led me over to the merry-go-round. He stepped onto it, turned, then held out his hand to help me up. I reached out for his hand as I climbed on. We walked over to the center of the merry-go-round and lay down, our arms intertwined, while we watched the faint outline of the clouds glide across the sky in silence. Moments passed for what seemed like a lifetime, when finally Dustin spoke.

"Hey, Sam..."

I turned my head to look at him and replied, "Yeah, Dustin?"

"Do you see that?" he asked as he pointed up towards the night sky.

I looked from him to the sky questionably, not sure exactly what I was supposed to be seeing. "I'm not exactly sure what you are trying to show me, babe."

"It's Columba, which means dove. See, it's there just below Orion, the hunter, and to the west of Puppis, which is the Stern of Argo, the Ship."

Dustin pointed at where Orion and Puppis were so I would be able to find Columba.

"Oh, now I see. But why did you pick that constellation to show me?"

Dustin turned his body to face me and he held my hand closer to him as he gazed into my eyes with certainty as he answered, "Because a dove is a symbol of peace and that is what I will provide for you in your life."

He then gazed admiringly into my eyes for what seemed like forever before he leaned in and kissed me on the forehead. I was speechless. All I did was smile up at him as we lay together on the merry-go-round, wrapped deep in each other's arms.

Around nine o'clock, Mr. James called Dustin to let us know that they were ready to go back to the cabin, and wanted us to meet them at the truck in half an hour. We got up and off the merry-go-round and headed back into town to meet Dustin's parents at the truck, and rode back to the cabin.

All of us got up early the next morning, for we were all going to see the Cumberland Falls. We hiked up the trail to the falls, listening to the sounds of the rustle of the wind, birds singing, and the faint roar of the falls in the distance. Seeing the mightiness of the falls as they crashed over and down onto the rocks below reminded me of the possibility of a greater power beyond this earth. A sense of peace and comfort overcame me as I closed my eyes and held out my arms like wings, listening to the sound of each water drop, whistle of the wind, and bird's chirp. I felt like I was flying over the falls, watching everything from below, leaving everything behind.

I heard the gentle voice of Dustin whisper in my ear, "Samantha, baby..."

I opened my eyes to the sound of his voice to find his body up against mine, hands linked with mine, and his chin resting on my shoulder.

"I love you, Samantha."

I turned into his body, embracing his scent.

"I love you too, Dustin."

Dustin smiled his mysterious grin as he cradled me in his arms, the two of us together looking beyond. Together we admired the magnificent beauty for what felt like an eternity.

We headed back home the following morning ready to take another swing at true reality, a chance at a fresh start on life as a freshman and junior in college at Kansas State University.

—ᘻ—

July 18, 2023 at 7:13 p.m.

The time with the James family was just amazing! I had such a good time. It was nice being able to relax and have some fun time with the family.

Dustin was so sweet during the trip, as he always is. I thought the consolation thing was adorable. He is such a gentleman. I can't wait until next year!

I hope someday I'll become a part of this family... aka married to Dustin!

Sincerely,

Samantha Bennett

Chapter 6

BROTHERLY LOVE

Love must be sincere...Be devoted to one another in brotherly love.
—ROMANS 12:9–10

S UMMER WAS ABOUT to end and a new year of
school was about to begin; only this time I
would be going to college, not high school.
Boxes full of school supplies, apartment necessities,
and clothes were stacked up in piles by the back
door, waiting to be brought out and into the bed of
the truck. As the move-in day drew closer, the boxes
moved from the back door to the bed of the truck,
and the trailer was loaded with tack, feed, horse
kits, and eventually horses. We headed to Kansas
State University, where Dustin would continue his
education in veterinary medicine and I would begin
my education in family studies and human services.

We arrived in Manhattan, Kansas a few hours
later, and stopped on the outskirts to drop off
Guardian and Debonair at Silent Winds Horse Farm.
After leaving the horses and trailer, Dustin and I
went into town, stopping to pick up a pizza to share
before heading to the hotel for the night.

I opened the door to our room, walked in, and set
my overnight bag on one of the beds. Dustin came
in right behind me carrying his bag and the pizza.
He set his bag next to the other bed, and placed the
pizza box on the bed.

"Mmm...man, that pizza smells tasty," I said as I
plopped beside Dustin.

"Ha-ha, you must be really hungry, Sam. Then
again, we don't get pizza that often."

"True."

We cuddled with each other as we ate the pizza
and watched TV. Once we both were too full to eat
one more piece of pizza, Dustin got up and placed
the cardboard box on the desk, then came back to

his bed. He wrapped his arm around me, stroking my hair as we lay on the bed. I rested my head against his chest, listening to the beat of his heart and the sound of his breathing. His hands gently brushed through my hair, careful not to be too hard around the bruises on the side of my face and neck. After about an hour, we decided to turn off the TV and get ready for bed.

"Hey, babe, do you need help putting on the lotion for your cuts and bruises?"

"Yeah, just my back, shoulders, and the back of my neck, though."

"OK, just let me know when you're ready."

"OK."

As I began to slowly, gingerly undress and put the lotion on in the bathroom, I saw another girl looking back at me in the mirror, a girl I couldn't recognize. She was covered from head to foot in yellow, green, and blue bruises, scars, and slowly healing wounds. Her eyes were deep with sorrow, calling for help; only I couldn't help her. I put my pajama pants on and called out to Dustin to come help me put the lotion on my back. Dustin opened the bathroom door and walked in barefoot and shirtless. I handed him the lotion, then turned my back to him. Through the mirror, I could see the pain and sorrow in his eyes. He squeezed lotion in his hands and very gently and cautiously rubbed it into my battered back. Every now and then he would hit a tender spot and I would wince and moan.

"Sorry, baby, I'll try and go gentler."

A few minutes later he set the lotion on the

counter, lightly rested his hands on my shoulders, and leaned in to give me a kiss on the cheek.

"All finished."

I slightly turned my head towards him and said, "Thanks, babe."

He smiled and turned, heading out of the bathroom, and shut the door behind him. I put my shirt on then walked back into the bedroom and crawled into my bed.

"Night, Dustin, love you."

"Goodnight, Sam, love you."

The next morning Dustin and I got up, checked out of the hotel, and drove to our apartment complex. When we arrived at the apartment the movers had already brought our belongings and furniture into the rooms. It took Dustin and me a few hours to unload the truck, but before long we were all moved in and settled. Dustin and I plopped onto the couch exhausted.

"Man, I'm beat and starved. I don't want to get up, but I have to if we want to get food," Dustin childishly complained.

I looked at him and laughed. "Yeah, we need to get groceries to be able to make some lunch, or go eat somewhere."

"Fine, let's grab some food then go grocery shopping so we can just chill. Later we can walk around town and maybe take a stroll through the campus."

"OK, let's go!"

We locked our apartment and walked down to the parking lot, got into the truck, and drove into town. We ate at a sandwich shop in the downtown area then went shopping for groceries and necessities. As we were wandering up and down the aisles, one of Dustin's friends from school saw us and came over to chat. He was a muscled cowboy of average height with short blonde hair and light blue eyes.

He reached out to clasp Dustin's hand and give him one of those "brotherly hugs."

"Hey, Dustin, how've you been?"

"Hey Keith! Pretty good, staying busy with the farm and settling into the apartment with Samantha."

"Oh, yeah, you mentioned that."

Keith turned to me and extended his hand.

"Hi, I'm Keith; as you are well aware."

I grinned out of amusement and replied, "Yeah, I'm Samantha."

"Well, Dustin, I best be going. I'll see you around. Nice to finally meet you, Samantha."

Keith continued on his way down the aisle, only to turn back around and yell, "Oh, hey, I'm having a beginning-of-the-year party at my place tomorrow around four in the afternoon if you'd like to come."

"Yeah, sure, we might stop by. See you later, then," Dustin yelled.

Keith left the aisle and Dustin and I were left with only the sound of squeaky shoes and carts.

"So, I'm assuming you know Keith from school."

"Yeah, we've had a couple of classes together."

"Oh, I see. That's cool."

"Yep."

We finished our shopping and headed back to the apartment. We unpacked and lounged around for the rest of the evening. The following morning, I awoke to the smell of blueberry pancakes, bacon, and freshly brewed coffee. I walked into the kitchen, still half asleep and in my pajamas, and sure enough there was Dustin, dressed in a muscle tank and his boxers, making breakfast. He glanced up and turned around the stove, smiling at me.

"Well, good morning sleepyhead. I thought I would make some of my famous pancakes for a homewarming surprise."

I smiled, and replied, "Mornin', smells good. Need help?"

"Nope just sit right there at the bar. Would you like some orange juice or coffee?"

"Orange juice, please."

"Okeydoke, just a second."

The pancakes sizzled on the griddle and the smell of greasy bacon seeped through the oven. It was making my mouth water and my stomach growl.
"Ha-ha, sounds like someone's hungry," Dustin commented as he placed the pancakes on two plates and pulled the bacon from the oven. I swear I could see the grease sizzling as the hot bacon hit the room-temperature air. Dustin set this decadent plate of pancakes with fresh blueberries and strawberries and bacon on the table, with a glass of orange juice sitting right next to it.

"Here you go, a hearty breakfast just for you and me."

"Ah, thanks, babe, just the way I like it."

I leaned in towards Dustin and gave him a soft kiss on the cheek.

He blushed then said, "Aw, shucks. Anything for my Samantha."

I laughed then started to eat.

"So, what are you doing today?" I asked Dustin curiously.

"Well, I thought I'd go ride Debonair, then probably stop by Keith's house to say hi. Want to come?"

"OK, I'd love to see Guardian and take him for a run. Plus, it would be nice to meet some of your friends officially."

"OK, sounds like a plan. Shall we leave after breakfast?"

"Sounds good."

We finished breakfast and headed out to Silent Winds. Dustin and I tacked up Debonair and Guardian and took off up the trail towards the river. Racing through the woods, dodging the trees up the trail, we made it to the river's edge. We dismounted and tied our horses to one of the tree branches, then we lay out in the sun on the riverbank, watching the clouds drift by to the sound of the flowing water. I must have fallen asleep because I found myself waking up under the warmth of the sun and Dustin's jean jacket. I looked around trying to find out where he had gone. However, I didn't have to look for very long. Dustin came walking back from the horses and knelt beside me; his arm stretched out, gently brushing his rough hand across the side of my face.

"Hey babe, did you have a nice nap?"

I gazed up at him, memorized by his big, warm, dark brown eyes before I replied, "Yeah. How long was I out?"

He softly laughed in his deep voice as he said, "Long enough to leave dirt and grass imprints on the side of your face."

I sat up, startled. "What? Are you serious?"

"Ha-ha, yes I am serious, but I brushed off most of the dirt. You know what would take off the rest?"

"What?" I asked urgently.

He laughed his soft, devious laugh, leaned in towards my ear and whispered, "Water."

I leaned away from his face, looking at him with suspicion. "You wouldn't dare."

"Oh, yes I would...."

He jumped to his feet and ran at me, picked me up off the ground, and carried me into the river.

I tried to yell, "Dustin, let—me—go!" but I kept laughing and screaming. I tried to wiggle out of his grip, yet there was no point.

He dropped me into the river. I stood back up in the water and glared at him.

"How dare you? I'm all wet!"

"Ha-ha, so?" he said with a mischievous smile.

I smiled back, "So, that means payback."

He looked at me surprised. "Really? How so?"

A smile crept up my face.

"Like this!" I bent down, putting my hands under the water behind me, and then brought my hand forward, throwing the water at Dustin.

He took a step back, protecting his face with his hands; only that didn't really do much, since he fell backwards into the river.

When the water stilled around him, I saw a look of surprise written all over his face...then a smile... followed by laughter.

"Good shot, but not good enough."

"Really? I'm not the one lying in the river."

"At least not at the moment...."

Dustin jumped up and ran over towards me. I laughed and turned to run away from him. A few lunges and laughs later, however, Dustin caught up to me and tackled me. The water splashed up and over us. When I looked up I saw Dustin's face glistening, under the ray of sunlight, over me. The white undershirt he was wearing emphasized his muscles as the water on the shirt drenched his body.

"Gotcha," Dustin said with a smirk.

"Yeah, well, I got you first," I teased.

Dustin rolled off of me and got up, turning back around to give me a hand. We trudged through the water to the bank and headed back to the barn. As he walked the horses down to the pasture, Dustin asked me if I still wanted to go to Keith's house for the party.

"Yeah, sure."

"OK, we can leave around 3:45 this afternoon."

"OK, sounds good."

We placed Debonair and Guardian in the pasture and headed back to the truck and drove back into town, to the apartment.

As we walked into the apartment, Dustin's phone rang.

"Hello?"

"Hey, Dustin, it's Keith!"

"Oh, hey Keith, what's up?"

"Nothing much, just getting stuff ready for the party. Are you coming?"

"Yeah, Sam and I both are."

"Awesome! Hey, you wouldn't mind picking up some bags of ice, would you?"

"No, how many do you need?"

"Oh, probably just two or three would be fine."

"OK, we will pick some up on our way to your house. Sam and I should be there a little after four, then."

"OK, sounds good. See you then."

"OK, bye, Keith!"

"Bye, Dustin!"

Dustin hung up the phone as he ambled into the kitchen where I was making some sandwiches for lunch.

"Who was that?" I asked.

"Keith. He was asking if we were coming to the party, and if we could pick up some ice on the way to his house."

"Oh, so I'm guessing we are picking up ice?"

"Yeah, ha-ha, guess we are. We should probably leave around 3:30."

"OK. Can we eat these sandwiches I made first?"

Dustin made a devious face and said, "Of course!" as he came around the counter, grabbed the plate with the sandwich from my hands, and gave me a kiss on the cheek.

I was so surprised that I stood speechless for a second before I busted out laughing. Dustin sat on a stool at the kitchen counter smiling his mischievous smile at me as he devoured his sandwich. A little after 3:30, we proceeded out the door to stop at the supermarket for ice on our way to Keith's house.

Dustin turned onto Keith's street, and stopped halfway down the street from Keith's house. We heard music blaring through the open door and windows and out into the street. People streamed out into the front yard, and there was a mess of beer cans already sprawled all over the front lawn.

"Um...is that Keith's house?" I asked Dustin nervously.

Dustin sat in silence with his mouth slightly open for a second before he replied, "Uh...yeah."

"Are we still going to go?"

"Why don't we just drop off the ice and say hi to Keith, since we told him we were coming, and then leave?"

"OK," I agreed, although I wasn't really reassured.

Dustin put the truck in park and turned to me, looking into my eyes with concern.

"Samantha, I want you to stay close to me, OK?"

"OK."

I really didn't mind. I was planning on staying close to him anyway. Dustin took my hand and led me to the house while he carried the ice in his other hand. Following Dustin's lead, I very cautiously stepped through the crowd and mess of trash. I heard people calling out Dustin's name, but he didn't pay any mind. I think he just wanted to get in and out of there, as I did. Surprisingly, we made it through and into the house. It was twice as crowded as it was outside, and it reeked of beer, cigarette smoke, and what I believe were other drugs.

There were people everywhere. With every step I took I ran into someone. Dustin tried to yell out for Keith, but over the blaring music and people talking and screaming, he didn't have much luck. Finally, we made it to the kitchen, where Dustin saw tubs of ice-filled coolers with beer. He handed me one of the ice bags and we ripped them open and poured the bags into the coolers, assuming that was where the ice was supposed to go.

"Duuuude, Dustin, you made it!"

Dustin looked up and saw Keith leaning against the kitchen door trying to walk towards us. He looked high and drunk, with red bloodshot eyes; he wasn't even walking or talking straight. I clutched Dustin's arm as Keith made his way towards us.

"IIII thhhhought you werrren't goin' to show."

"Well, as you can see, or maybe not, we did, and brought ice like you asked. And we are going to be leaving now."

"Aw, come on, Bro, you jjjjuuusssstt got here. Stay and chill for awhile. Be a gennntllllemannnn and show your lady friend what we do at parties."

Keith, by this time, was right in front of me. I started taking steps back, for he was really invading my personal bubble; not to mention that he reeked profusely of beer and it was making me gag and my eyes water.

Dustin grabbed Keith's arm and said firmly, "Man, back off."

"Alright, alright, alright! Let go!"

Once Keith had backed up, Dustin let go of him. I still didn't trust him. There's something about drugs and beer that changes people, even if they don't admit or know it. Plus, even though Keith had backed off and calmed down, he still had that look in his eye...a look I will never forget.

"Keith, whatever happened to a small back-to-school party?" Dustin asked, concerned.

"Wwwhat do you mean? This is a grrreat party. Don't you like it? Or is your girl...uncomfortable?"

I didn't like the way he said "uncomfortable." It was really creepy.

Dustin's back stiffened and he stood up straighter, moving in front of me.

"What's that supposed to mean?" Dustin uttered protectively.

Leaning against the kitchen counter, Keith very casually replied, "Oh, just that she looks uptight is all. Maybe you should give her a few beers and loosen her up some. Or maybe, if you'd like, I can help with that."

I couldn't believe what he said, and neither could Dustin. Rage filled Dustin's eyes. He strutted towards Keith and before Keith could realize what was happening Dustin grabbed his shirt and punched him in the face, knocking him to the floor.

As he was lying on the floor with a busted lip, still half-dazed and confused, Keith asked, "Dude, what was that for? It was just an offer."

Dustin towered over Keith, looking down at him with menacing eyes, and said, "Don't you ever say anything like that to Sam or anyone else, or you will have to deal with me. You hear?"

"Yeah, OK!"

"Good." Dustin turned to me, holding out his hand as he said, "Come on Sam, let's go home."

I stood astounded and in shock for a second, then I reached out for Dustin's hand. We walked very quickly through the now-quiet crowd and made it back to the truck. Dustin led me to the passenger-side door and waited for me to get inside before he shut the door behind him, and jumped into the driver's side door. Before he put the truck into drive, he placed his hand on my knee and with those chocolate-brown, concerned eyes, gave me a side glace as he asked quietly, "You OK?"

I smiled and softly answered, "Yeah, I am."

He smiled contently, then put the truck into drive and we headed back to the apartment.

—⁓⁓—

August 31, 2023 at 12:13 p.m.

Dear Diary,

The first week of school is going pretty well if I do say so myself, ha-ha. The classes this semester aren't too hard, or at least not yet, but I'm not too worried about it. It's amazing how many organizations there are for you to get involved in. They have a little bit of everything and you can even create a club/organization if you want to. I have a feeling the years here will go by very fast.

Dustin has been pretty busy. With classes and work just starting, we haven't seen much of each other. Although, Guardian keeps me company. He and Debonair are both doing very well at the boarding farm. They quite enjoy it, but it's not like home.

After the incident at Keith's house, Dustin hasn't called or mentioned him. Keith stopped by a few times when we weren't here, and left notes on the door apologizing and asking to talk. But I think it will be a while before Dustin is willing to speak to Keith again. Personally, I feel kind of bad for Keith, but at the same time I don't. I mean, he was really asking for it when he said those things—I don't care if his excuse was that he was drunk and high—it was wrong. It really freaked me out the way he was acting, but I am so glad I have a boyfriend who cares and loves me for all the right reasons. Dustin is the best big-brother-boyfriend ever!

Well, I got to go make lunch. Talk to you soon.

Samantha Bennett

Chapter 7

FREE FALL

*Praise be to the God and Father of our Lord
Jesus Christ, the Father of compassion and the
God of all comfort, who comforts us in all our
troubles, so that we can comfort those in any
trouble with the comfort we ourselves have
received from God.*

—2 CORINTHIANS 1:3–4

D USTIN AND I are taking Debonair to the Twelfth Annual Green Rivers Three-Day Eventing Show this weekend. I've been conditioning Debonair by slowly working his way up to training level with flat work in the dressage ring, fence jumping in the arena up to roughly 3 feet 6 inches for stadium and cross country, and working on his endurance on the trail. Debonair and I have been building up our confidence for this show since we competed in it a year ago.

We left for the competition on Tuesday afternoon and arrived at the grounds early Thursday morning. As we pulled into the driveway with the windows down, the smells of the horses, hay, and horse manure filled the truck. I inhaled and exhaled with a big sigh and a smile. Dustin looked at me like I was crazy and laughed. His facial expression was priceless! When I looked over at him after realizing he was looking at me and saw his expression I just broke up laughing.

"Ha-ha, OK. Somebody's off her rocker," Dustin said amusingly as he continued down the gravel road to find a place to park.

"I think you are the one off your rocker. Can't you smell those wonderful aromas? It brings back so many memories."

"Yeah, I guess, but I don't think it's worth the exaggerated breathing. I mean, you inhaled and exhaled like you had just walked into the kitchen and smelled a freshly baked pan of chocolate chip cookies. I don't think this smell measures up to that, especially not to your cookies."

Dustin blushed and flashed one of his signature

boyish smiles as he glanced at me through the corner of his eye.

I blushed out of embarrassment as I responded, "Aw, really? You're too sweet. Thanks Dustin."

By this time he had parked the truck and trailer. He leaned over the armrest and gave me a tender, soft kiss on the cheek.

"Any time, babe," he said with a sincere tone, his glistening, soft eyes looking deep beyond my soul.

We got out of the truck and unloaded shavings and buckets for Debonair's stall. I spread the shavings around the stall and put the feeding bucket up while Dustin filled up two of the buckets of water. Once the stall was fit for a king, I unloaded Debonair and took him for a stroll to graze. After an hour I put Debonair in his stall to feed him and put him up for the night.

Dustin, a few friends and I had a cookout with hot dogs and burgers by the trailer that evening. We surrounded ourselves around the crackling sounds and smoky aroma of the warm, open fire. We enjoyed the time together, devouring the hot dogs and burgers, socializing, and laughing over the good times. Soon everybody left to check on their horses one last time before the morning and hit the hay, as did Dustin and I. It seemed like right when I closed my eyes, I heard Dustin softly whispering my name and felt his rough hand gently stroking my back. I slowly rolled over and opened my eyes to see Dustin leaning over the sofa and smiling his warm, boyish grin.

"Good morning, time to get up," he softly spoke.

I groaned, and went to feed Debonair while

Dustin set out cereal and fruit for breakfast. When I came back to the trailer, Dustin had everything set up and was standing behind a chair, which he had pulled out for me.

"My lady, your breakfast is served," Dustin said proudly with a big grin.

A big smile crept up my face. "Why thank you, sir," I replied as I sat down in the chair.

Dustin and I enjoyed our breakfast together, then I was off to get myself ready for our dressage competition, while Dustin took Debonair for a walk. Once Debonair was all tacked up, we headed to the warm-up area. I mounted Debonair and began to warm up both him and myself at the warm-up arena. After a good thirty minutes I gave Debonair his neck and let him stretch out at a walking pace around the warm-up area. I stopped by where Dustin was standing to get my dressage test so I could look over it one last time.

"So, Debonair looks very good out there," Dustin commented.

"Yeah, I agree, he's doing very well. He was a little fresh in the beginning, but that's expected."

I skimmed over the test for about five minutes or so, then I continued walking Debonair around until it was time for us to begin the test. We trotted around the ring until the judge rang the bell. Together Debonair and I trotted down the center of the ring, saluted the judge, and then continued on with our test with elegance and ease, ending with another perfect salute to the judge. I exited the ring and walked Debonair by a shaded tree, where Dustin was standing with a big smile on his face.

I dismounted Debonair and began putting up the stirrups and loosening his girth. Dustin came up behind me and wrapped his arms securely around me, resting his chin on my shoulder.

"You guys were amazing!" Dustin pointed out as he began cradling me back and forth.

"Yeah, Debonair is the best, and so is Guardian!" I agreed with a smile as I kissed Dustin's rough, stubbled cheek.

"You all are! End of discussion. Now let's go have some lunch," Dustin argued with a laugh.

I laughed with a sigh in agreement, and together all three of us walked back to the trailers to untack, and then to the stalls to put Debonair up until stadium jumping.

For lunch Dustin and I had ham and turkey sandwiches with a vegetable tray and some chips, with some of Mrs. James's famous lemonade-tea. Dustin fancied putting the lunch into a picnic basket he had apparently brought, and suggested that we eat under one of the shade trees by the stadium ring and have a lunch-and-show type of meal, which I thought was quite sweet and enjoyed. We ate and watched the stadium jumping competition for about an hour and a half before I left to walk the course for my division. After I walked the course a few times, I came back to the stall to find Debonair all nice and clean with his saddle on. I stopped for a second, taking in what I was seeing, then went over to the trailer where I found Dustin getting Debonair's jumping boots and bridle.

"Hey, I see that Debonair is all ready to go."

"Yeah, I thought I could get him ready for you; that

way you wouldn't have to rush, so you could focus on the course."

"Aw, that's so sweet, thank you." I gave Dustin a hug then headed into the trailer to clean up a bit and get ready for Stadium Jumping. I came out a few minutes later, grabbed my jumping crop, gloves, and helmet, and followed Dustin and Debonair to the jumping warm-up ring. I mounted Debonair and went off to warm up. After a few times each direction of flat work and jumping Debonair over the three jumps a few times, I gave him a break and walked him around the ring until it was about time for us to go up to the stadium ring. We stood outside the ring waiting for the rider ahead of us to finish the course. Dustin came up beside us, patted Debonair on the neck, and then looked up at me.

"You guys are going to do great!" he said reassuringly.

"Thanks."

A minute later the competitor before me finished, and I went into the arena. With precision, accuracy, and grace Debonair jumped over each obstacle with ease. It was a clear round! I was so proud of Debonair! Now we just had to give it all we have tomorrow at cross-country. I untacked and hosed down Debonair, and put him back in his stall. By the time I closed the gate to the stall, Dustin had come back from checking the scores. He embraced my body around him. I smelled the faint scent of a mixture of Old Spice and the smell of the horses coming from Dustin's sweaty body as I pressed into him.

"Hey, Sam, guess what?" he said with an excited, teasing tone.

"What?" I said eagerly as I turned my head to look at him.

"You and Debonair are third in your division."

I jumped out from his grasp and started to somewhat yell, "Oh, my gosh, are you serious?"

Dustin had a look of complete disownment of me written all over his face before he broke with laughter, saying, "Yes, Samantha, I am serious."

I couldn't believe it! We were in third place! I started jumping up and down with such excitement that the other competitors looked at me like I was some crazy mad woman, but I didn't care. I ran and leaped into Dustin's arms, giving him a big kiss on his manly lips. Then, I was so overjoyed and proud of Debonair that I ran into his stall and gave him a humongous bear hug around the neck.

Dustin was so amused by my reaction that he got the camera from the trailer and must have taken a picture of me with Debonair, for I heard the sound of a camera and turned to see him holding it. Although, I don't believe he meant for me to catch him with it, because his facial expression was like watching a child who had just been caught taking a cookie from the cookie jar.

An awkward silence crept over us and then we both busted out laughing. Together we walked hand in hand up to the arena to watch some more stadium jumping and meet up with some friends. A couple hours later I went back to the stables to bring Debonair out for some grass and to stretch his legs.

We were out chilling out under one of the big shaded trees when I noticed that a little girl's horse was starting to act up in the warm-up area. First, the horse started prancing around and going in circles. The instructor yelled at the poor girl, telling her to stop her horse, but I could tell that the poor girl was starting to get scared. I was surprised that the instructor and all the people around the girl were just standing around. The horse kept prancing around and wouldn't listen to the girl, no matter what she tried to do.

Finally, after ten minutes or so, she seemed to have calmed her horse down—or at least it was able to start jumping over the fences again. She went through the jumps twice and on the third go-around, the horse approached and jumped with no problem. However, when he landed back onto the ground he bolted out of the warm-up area. Everyone was screaming and yelling at the girl to stop her horse and running after her trying to stop it, but in spite of their efforts no one was able to catch up to the girl. The horse took off towards the woods with the little girl clinging on for dear life, her face full of terror and fear.

I jumped onto Debonair and took off after the girl at full gallop. I could faintly hear people yelling, "Hey what are you doing? Go save her!" All I could think of was catching up to the girl and wishing people would get out of my way. Everything became a blur, and soon I could see the girl still hanging on in the distance. I saw a shortcut that would bring me right behind the girl. I quickly turned Debonair down the trail galloping at full force. I saw a prelim brush jump up ahead. I was thinking, *we are so close; we can't turn back now.* Then, out of nowhere, I heard my mother's voice.

"Samantha, my child, *go!*"

So, instead of turning back, I got Debonair collected and balanced for the brush, stood in a two-point and focused on this tree just beyond the brush. We became ever closer to the jump. Everything around me vanished and all I could see was the jump and the tree and all I could hear was Debonair's hooves pound the ground with every stride and breath he took. As we got closer I leaned in closer to Debonair and whispered to him, *inena, iginvtli,* which my mother taught me means, *Let's go, my brother.* Debonair's ears perked forward, his neck arched, and I felt his body transition to a whole new gear as he leaped into the air. In midair over the jump, everything seemed to freeze or slow down in time. Flying down to the ground, all I could hear were the individual sounds of each of Debonair's hooves hitting the ground.

As one we flew through the sky and beyond. I saw the little girl out of the corner of my eye. I directed Debonair towards the little girl, and came up behind and then beside her. The girl looked at me with desperation and fear.

I reached out to her and mouthed, *Jump!*

The little girl looked at the ground, then at me with uncertainty. I reassured her that I would not let her fall. The girl let go of her saddle and reached out for me as she lunged out of her saddle and into my arms.

"Whoa!" I told Debonair.

Debonair slowed to a stop. The girl clutched to my body shaking, crying, and wailing out of exhaustion, relief, and fear. I cradled and hummed to the girl, trying to calm her down. A few minutes later, Dustin came up behind us with a group of riders.

"Are y'all OK?" Dustin asked as they started to slow.

"Yeah, we are. Her horse kept going that way into the woods." I pointed.

"OK, thanks."

They took off, continuing onward into the woods, while Debonair and I with the girl turned around and walked back to the show grounds. When we came out of the woods and back into view, people started to cheer when they saw that the girl was OK. Debonair stopped and the girl lifted up her head, looking up at me with her tear-stained face. Her face lit up when she saw her parents running up to us. She stretched out to her mother. Seeing both her mother and father taking her into their arms, crying and hugging her with relief that their daughter was OK was enough of a reward for me.

The father came up to me with tears of joy flowing from his eyes. He approached Debonair, stroking him on the neck and then approached me, placing his hand lightly on my thigh. He looked up at me and said through his sobs, "Thank you."

I smiled and nodded. The father and mother turned and started walking away, carrying their little girl back to the trailers. The little girl lifted her head from her mother's shoulder, looked at me with a big smile, and lifted one of her little hands from around her mother and waved at me. I smiled back and waved back to her as they disappeared into the distance.

I dismounted and started to lead Debonair to the wash racks, when I saw out of the corner of my eye Dustin and the other riders bringing the girl's horse back from the woods. I smiled contentedly and continued down to the wash racks.

A few minutes later Dustin came by the wash racks. He looked tired and frustrated about something.

"Hey, how's the girl's horse?" I asked concerned as I continued hosing Debonair down.

"He's fine. Still a little wound up and a little tired. The vet is looking him over now to see if he can find out the cause. How are you and Debonair?"

"We are good." I paused. "Debonair and I cleared the prelim brush in the back."

Dustin froze and looked at me in disbelief.

"Are you serious?"

"Yeah, it was the shortest way to get to the girl, and I didn't know it was back there until I saw it ahead of me. I was going to turn around or go off the trail, but I heard my mother. She told me to go on."

He was silent for a second or two, taking in what I had said. "Wow."

That's all he said, "Wow." Then again, what do you say after hearing what I had just told him? We stood in silence listening to the birds and the water run. After hosing Debonair down I placed him in his stall.

Throughout he rest of the day, people continuously came up to me congratulating and thanking me—which I didn't really mind, but I felt I wasn't the only one who should be taking the credit. After a while, things started to quiet down. By the next morning things seemed to be back to somewhat normal.

During most of the morning I was able to feed and get Debonair ready for our cross-country run without being pestered by people. However, when the announcer called out my name, everybody started to cheer and yell. I'm guessing sometime throughout the night people found out who I was— which I didn't mind, I guess.

The ten-second mark came around as I went into the starting box.

"10, 9, 8, 7, 6, 5, 4, 3, 2, 1, 0. Good luck!" the person at the start box said.

Debonair took off over and through the course with speed and precision. Taking every jump in stride, we went over logs, ditches, and jumps of all kinds, through water, and down banks. With no refusals, we finished in a decent time.

By the afternoon the show was over and the awards were being given out; we had won the training division. . Near the end, just as people started to leave, one of the judges called out to the audience, "Wait, there is one more award!"

The people stopped and started to mumble, wondering what this award could be. The judge began, "Yesterday, as we all are aware, a rider went after a little girl and her horse even though she endangered her own life. Well, we know they both returned safe and unharmed. So I present this bouquet of flowers to the young rider, Miss Samantha Bennett."

Everybody cheered, clapped, and whistled while I

stood astounded, not expecting anything like what had just happened. After about a second or two, I walked up in joyful tears to the judge and was handed the flowers. People came up to me to congratulate and thank me one by one. Finally, Dustin and I were able to go and start loading everything up to go back home. While Dustin put the last bit of our belongings in the trailer, I wrapped Debonair in his shipping boots. As I was loading Debonair into the trailer and locking everything up before we headed out, Dustin saw the little girl come running up the gravel road behind me.

"Hey Sam, look." Dustin pointed behind me.

I turned around and saw the little girl running up towards me with something in her hand. I knelt to the ground and waited for her to come to me.

"Wait, wait, this is for you," she said, trying to catch her breath.

The girl held out a piece of paper that had a hand-drawn picture of her and me on, I think, Debonair.

The note read, "Thank you Debonair and Samantha for saving my life. Your friend, Grace."

I looked up from the note, tears trickling down my face.

"Thank you, Grace."

Grace smiled and gave me a big hug, then turned and ran back to her trailer, stopping halfway and turning back around to wave. I waved back and watched her run back down the road as I stood in Dustin's arms.

January 15, 2025 at 9:45 a.m.

Dear Diary,

The show this past weekend was by far the most exciting, interesting, and rewarding one I've ever been to. Debonair was amazing during all his events, which I am very proud of him for. When we went after that little girl, we were linked as one body. When I saw that prelim brush jump, I was thinking, "Oh, no, what are we going to do?" I mean, we could have turned around, but we would have been further behind the girl then we already were. I think Debonair knew what we were doing; I just needed that reassurance that everything was going to be OK. When we jumped over the prelim jump it felt like we were going in slow motion—so slow, it felt like we were flying.

When we caught up to the girl and she was clinging to my arms for dear life, I felt a sense of mothering to the child. Watching her walk away in her parents' arms, I knew she had a life worth living, one far greater than my own, with her mother and father. Knowing that she was going to be OK was more than enough of a reward for me. When I received those flowers I felt as though I didn't deserve them. I mean, no one was helping her when she was crying out for help and, knowing how that feels, I just had to go help her. Knowing that she is now safe and sound with her mother and father is more of a comfort for me than anything else.

Well, after this exciting weekend, Dustin and I will head back to Manhattan to pick up Guardian and go back to Kentucky for Christmas Break.

Sincerely,

Samantha Bennett

Chapter 8

SOFT LIPS; NO VALUES

So do not fear, for I am with you; do not be dismayed, for I am your God. I will strengthen you and help you; I will uphold you with my righteous right hand ... For I am the LORD, your God, who takes hold of your right hand and says to you, Do not fear; I will help you.

—ISAIAH 41:10–13

A LITTLE AFTER FIVE o'clock on a cool spring morning, Dustin and I were doing some barn chores while we waited for Guardian and Debonair to finish their grain so we could go for a ride. We cleaned some tack, organized the tack room, and moved some hay and feed from the storing shed into the feed room. Around six thirty we headed out of the barn and hit the trails. We raced through Moccasin Valley and up Cougar Mountain, heading to Heaven's Peak to watch the sunrise. We reached Heaven's Peak just as the sun was peaking over the hills in the distance. Dustin and I stood side by side, mounted on Debonair and Guardian under the oak tree, our hands linked together.

Once the sun positioned itself high enough in the sky for the day, Dustin and I headed back to the barn. We leisurely walked through the woods and across Big Bear Creek into Silent Deer Meadows. We both decided to stop there and let the horses graze for a while so we could watch the clouds in the sky. We dismounted Guardian and Debonair and walked onto the meadow and lay together in the grass, watching the clouds go by. After a while we got back on Guardian and Debonair and headed back.

"What a pretty sunrise, huh, baby?"

"Yes, I agree, Dustin."

I led Guardian into his stall after I un-tacked him and gave him some peppermint candies. I leaned against the barn door, waiting for Dustin to put Debonair away.

"Hurry up, Slow-Moe!" I teased.

I didn't hear a response for a little while, so I

headed back into the barn to look for Dustin. Out of nowhere he jumped from behind an empty stall and growled at me, then started chasing me. I skidded to a halt and spun around, screaming and laughing as I ran the other direction. He chased me out of the barn and about halfway between the barn and the house he caught up to me and tackled me to the ground. We rolled for a few feet, and when we stopped he was on top of me.

"Get off me, Dustin, you are suffocating me," I gasped.

"OK, babe," he laughed.

He started to get off of me, but he stopped halfway and gazed into my eyes. A smile crept up the side of his mouth. I looked at him puzzled, wondering what he was thinking about. Before that thought finished crossing my mind, he leaned in and kissed me tenderly on the lips. Our lips parted slowly, then we paused to admire one another.

"I love you," Dustin said.

"I love you too," I replied back.

He helped me up and we headed back to the house wrapped in each other's arms. We stepped through the screen door by the dining room. As we were walking through the dining room I cut Dustin off in mid-step as I turned to face him with my arms still wrapped around his warm body, resting my chin on his chest, looking into his warm, soft brown eyes. He smiled down at me as we stared deeply into each other's eyes.

"Hey, help me make some of the Famous James Homemade Chocolate Chip Cookies for Mr. and Mrs. Jenkins down the road... please," I begged.

He chuckled and replied, "Well, since you said please... of course."

I grinned ear to ear and jumped for joy as we headed towards the kitchen. The aroma of freshly baked cookies filled the kitchen air and floated throughout the house. The smells of the cookies were so tempting that they brought Mr. James out from his study and through the kitchen doors.

"Mmm...making cookies in here, are we?" Mr. James questioned.

Dustin and I looked at each other, surprised that his father had come out of his study, then started to laugh. Dustin turned to his father after a second to reply back.

"Yes, it was Samantha's idea to make our famous chocolate chip cookies for Mr. and Mrs. Jenkins down the road."

"That's nice. Make some extra for me and your mother, will you?"

"Of course," Dustin and I replied at the same time.

Mr. James sighed with a smile, shaking his head as he turned to go back into his study.

A few hours later the timer on the last batch of cookies went off. Dustin went to get a container for the cookies as I took the batch out of the oven. Dustin placed most of the cookies that were on the cooling rack into the container. I went over with one of the chocolate chip cookies, split it in half, and gave it to Dustin. He took it from my hand and placed it in his mouth. His eyes closed, a smile crept up his face, and his body began to sink as if the cookie were melting him from the inside as he chewed.

"We should *so* open our own bakery or something. These are amazing!"

I laughed. "You are more amazing."

He wrapped his arm around my waist and pulled me into his safe, warm body. He placed his other hand under my chin as he looked down into my eyes, smiling softly, and whispered, "You are more amazing than anything in the world to me." Then his soft "cookie" lips embraced mine.

"We'd better go deliver our cookies to Mr. and Mrs. Jenkins before it gets too late," I recommended.

"Aw, I guess that would be a good idea," he agreed.

We headed out the back and down the road hand-in-hand, with Yeller right behind us. Halfway down the road we were passing the old abandoned church on Faith Hill Drive when I noticed that Yeller had stopped and was growling a low growl.

"Dustin..." I motioned towards Yeller.

Dustin stopped and walked over to Yeller.

"What is it, boy? What do you see?"

Dustin looked around, trying to find out what Yeller was growling about. I started to get uneasy as they got closer to the church. I was just about to call out to them when I saw some movement in the bushes behind Dustin. My body froze and my heart started to race as I saw two men come from behind the bushes towards Dustin. I recognized one of the men, who had a blue plaid shirt on. Yeller ran at the men and started barking. Dustin turned around just as the man in the plaid shirt threw a punch at him, and the other man threw him against the church, knocking him unconscious. I screamed, dropping the cookies, and ran towards Dustin. Yeller chased the two men into the woods, nipping at their heels.

I knelt beside Dustin, crying as I attempted to wake him. I was so distraught in the chaos that I didn't hear the footsteps come up behind me. A hand covered my mouth and began to pull me away from Dustin. I thrashed and kicked, trying to get away, but whoever was behind me had a cloth in the hand over my mouth. Everything went fuzzy as I breathed in the fumes from the cloth. I reached out to Dustin, but he slipped away, along with the other surroundings.

When I awoke I was lying on a rough, worn area rug on a wooden floor. My father and the three men were all hovering over me. I began to scoot away from them, but my father quickly grabbed my leg so I couldn't go anywhere.

"You're not going anywhere, at least 'til we are through with you," he smirked.

My father motioned to the men to leave the room. They left one by one into another room that I couldn't exactly see. My father placed one of his hands next to my face ever so lightly to the floor. I moved my head from his hand to his face afraid of what was going through his mind. He leaned in towards me his hand moving up my leg as he went. He whispered in my ear...

"It's time."

My mind rushed with thoughts as I processed those words, trying to understand what he meant. Then I remembered that today was the anniversary of my mother's death. That only meant one thing....

My father lifted his hand off the floor and placed

in on my lower stomach. His rough, cold hands slid down my stomach, stopping at the brim of my jeans. They slowly began to unbutton my jeans, gliding down the zipper as they drifted further and further down.

Tears began to fall down my face and onto the floor.

"Please, no, I don't want...not again...please..." I sobbed pleadingly, but it didn't matter to him—it hadn't for each of the past six consecutive years either..

My father didn't hesitate or pause to consider what I had just said. His sickly horrendous mind was only focused on one thing and that was to make me pay for my mother. He forcefully pulled my jeans away from my body; then his hands proceeded to my pearl snap shirt. His hands ripped apart the shirt, exposing my bruised and scarred body. A smile of satisfaction crossed his face at his "accomplishments." Kneeling over me, he took off his stained old tank top muscle shirt, but he waited, admiring the moment, before he slowly pulled his jeans off. My insides screamed with pain and tears poured down my face. I've learned to just "go somewhere else" as this happens, as if I'm watching what is happening to me. After what felt like hours, my father lifted himself off my limp body, got dressed and left.

I wanted to run away, but my violated body was too weak. I lay on the floor fully exposed, not moving and quietly crying. Every hour or so for quite some time, one by one, the men of my father's "posse" came from the other room and used me as a "reliever" and a personal "punching bag."

I gingerly lifted my shattered, wounded body off the cold hard floor and reached for my clothes with piercing agony. After making sure my father and his followers were not coming out of the other room, I cautiously crawled for the open window across the room, dragging my damaged body behind me. I steadily, slowly hoisted my body up and through the window, gritting my teeth so I wouldn't scream from all of the pain. I fell onto the outside earth, and dragged my body to the trees up ahead of me. Once I had reached the trees, I gingerly leaned my aching body against one of the oak tree trunks. Closing my eyes from exhaustion, I prayed to God that He would save and protect me from Charles Bennett, my father.

As I began to pray, I entered a whole new world. This world wasn't like our world; it was full of luscious green forestry; the sun radiated down its glorious glow, and there was a feeling of peace and security about it. It was as if all pain and suffering had left me. I examined myself to see if these feelings were true, and when I lifted my shirt there were no bruises or scars, and no evidence of past or present broken bones. All of me was healed. As I lowered my shirt and raised my head, in the sunrays, I saw someone facing me down the path. He was dressed in a white-as-snow robe, had long, brown hair, and His arms were open wide. He walked towards me, His arms still open wide. Tears fell from my eyes. Were they of joy, fear, or happiness? I'm not exactly sure. A mix of emotions, I guess.

In all the emotional uproar, I collapsed to the ground. The man approached me, kneeling before me, wrapping His arms around me. A sense of safety and hominess came over me. He lifted me off the ground with ease and began carrying me down the path into the distance. I lifted my tear-stained face, admiring Him. As He walked with steady grace, He looked down at me smiling. His lips parted as He spoke...

"Don't worry, Samantha Elizabeth Bennett, I will protect you. You are safe now. I will never leave you."

Hearing those words brought relief and an invisible weight came off my shoulders. I looped my arms around His neck, resting my head on His chest and whispered...

"OK...Jesus...OK."

In the distance, I faintly heard hoofbeats and nickering. I looked up to Jesus with a questioning expression on my face. He gazed down at me in awe, answering my question with the words...

"I will never leave you, Samantha. I love you."

Parting with those last words, Jesus, along with His world, drifted from my grasp.

I could feel the earthly soil beneath me as I lay against the oak tree. The pain and weariness returned to my body, but I could feel a presence with me too. In the distance I could hear hoofbeats approaching closer and closer. I opened my eyes and saw Guardian drawing nearer to me. He halted next to me, lowering his head. I slowly reached for his mane and clasped onto him. He steadily hoisted me to my feet and stood patiently as I cautiously, steadily climbed onto his back. Clinging to his neck, my head resting against his mane, Guardian cantered into the sun with grace. With every stride I could faintly hear my father's cussing and yelling further and further away.

January 28, 2026 at 2:32 p.m.

Dear Diary,

I'm returning back home today after three weeks in the hospital. I don't really remember much of what has happened, except the past few days. Dustin told me that when he came around after being knocked out, he noticed I wasn't anywhere to be found. So, he ran back to the house and his parents rushed him to the hospital. They filed an endangered missing persons report with the police, then went back home to wait. However, the following day (three days after we were jumped), Dustin was on the porch home alone when he saw Guardian coming up the driveway with me dangling on top of him. He still isn't sure how Guardian got out, but I have an idea! The reason I don't remember this is because when he ran up to Guardian he found me unconscious, clothes inside out, torn, and stained with blood. He ran back to the house to get the truck and drove it up to Guardian, then jumped out, pulled me off Guardian, and carried me to the truck and rushed me to the hospital.

I woke up in the hospital twelve days later. Everything was so hazy; I didn't know where I was at first, but as things began to clear I saw Dustin by my bedside holding my hand with one hand and brushing my hair with the other. I remember him smiling at me and I remember smiling back, but then I must have fallen back asleep. Two days later I was awake and alert, but very sore. It seemed like my whole body was being stabbed with knives—even though I had morphine it didn't really seem to help. Hearing the extent of your injuries after something traumatic like that is really hard to grasp, especially when you're hearing it from someone else. I didn't want to believe what I was hearing. For nights on end, Dustin never left my side. Many times, halfway through the night I would wake up screaming and crying from such physical or emotional pain.

A few days later when the doctor thought I was in good enough condition to talk to the police, he let them come in and talk to me...which I wasn't! Hello, I was **raped** *and* **left for dead.** *Come on, who would want to relive a nightmare like that by telling it? It was hard emotionally, but slowly and surely I told them everything, and gave them the bag that I had asked Dustin to get from home a few days earlier (the one with the* photos and video footage). They left, and for five more days I stayed in the hospital. My friends, family, and even Yeller and Guardian visited me. Since I was on the first floor, I'm guessing while I was asleep, Dustin went and got Guardian; when I heard a tap on the window I woke and saw Dustin waving with Guardian by his side, peering through the window. One of the nurses slowly, cautiously lifted me from the bed and into the wheelchair and wheeled me outside to see him. It was one of the best days I had while I was at the hospital.

Now I'm coming back home, and will still be in a wheelchair for a few more weeks, though. I'll never forget, as we were heading out the front doors a nurse came up to me and said a policeman wanted to talk to me. He told me that my father had been arrested earlier that afternoon, and that they were planning to hold a hearing in April of this year. I couldn't believe it! I wanted to jump and scream, "Hurray!" But instead I just smiled, then started to bawl. I couldn't control it. For thirteen years I lived in fear and terror of one man and as of today, I don't have to anymore. I don't remember much of what happened after that, but now I'm home recuperating.

Samantha Bennett

Chapter 9

WITNESS 'TIL PROVEN GUILTY

*Be strong and courageous. Do not be terrified;
do not be discouraged, for the lord your God
will be with you wherever you go.*

—JOSHUA 1:9

I HATE THE WHOLE setting of court. I hate the whole idea—people stare at you in an intimidating way, you could hear a pen drop in the awkward silence, the weight of pressure is on you full force, and you have to face your enemy, even though that's who you've been trying to avoid your whole life.

The day came when I couldn't run from my father anymore, no matter how badly I wanted to. I sat anxiously on the bench outside the courtroom waiting for the hearing on my father's case. Dustin came over and knelt in front of me, dressed in his suit.

"Samantha, you're going to be just fine. Just answer the judge's and attorneys' questions truthfully and imagine that your father isn't there. I'll be in the pew right behind you supporting you all the way."

Dustin's dad came up behind him and said, "Dustin, it's time to go in."

"OK, thanks Dad. I love you, Samantha Elizabeth."

He rose up, kissed me on the forehead, and followed his dad through the double doors. I nervously waited in the quiet corridor for my attorney to come get me. Finally, after what felt like a lifetime, my attorney, Mr. Brett Matthews, came to get me. We walked through the double doors and down the aisle to the chairs and table up at the front. My eyes wandered around the courtroom, stopping the moment I saw a tall, muscled man with brown, buzzed hair and menacing gray eyes in an orange jumpsuit grinning right at me, along with three other men in jumpsuits. My heart began to race and I wanted to run the other direction, but I kept reminding myself, *He can't touch me, I'll be just fine, keep cool.* Brett and I sat in the chairs and waited for the judge to enter the courtroom.

The bailiff approached the court and yelled, "All rise!"

The door at the back opened and Judge Suzan Jenkins came out and sat in her seat.

"This court will come to order. Bailiff, can we have the first case?"

The bailiff approached the judge with the case file. She glanced at the file, then looked up at the court and said, "Prosecutor you may begin."

With that Brett stood up from his chair and said, "Thank you, Judge. Mr. Charles Wade Bennett is charged with the manslaughter of Mrs. Lillian Rose Bennett and the rape, child abuse, and attempted manslaughter of Samantha Elizabeth Bennett. Mr. Ray Kenneth Parker, Mr. Joe Henry Johnson, and Mr. Fred Matthew Williams are charged with the rape and attempted manslaughter of Samantha Elizabeth Bennett."

Judge Suzan Jenkins listened, then replied to Charles Bennett, Ray Parker, Joe Johnson, and Fred Williams's attorney, "Will the defendants please rise. You have heard the charges against you, and how do you plead?"

The attorney listened to the men then replied, "Not guilty, Your Honor."

The judge responded, "This will come to case on November 15, 2026. Dismissed"

Seven months later, the day came for the case. I was so nervous about testifying and just being in the same room as my father and the "posse."

Before Brett Matthews and I went in, he stopped to talk to me.

"Samantha, remember what we talked about and you will do just fine."

"Yeah, I remember. Do you have the bag I gave you?"

"Yes I do. Are you sure you want to be in the room when I show the video and pictures?"

"Yeah, I need to, for myself."

"OK, if you're sure. Are you ready to go in?"

"Ready as I'll ever be."

For a second time we walked through the double doors and down the aisle to wait in the chairs for the judge.

The bailiff approached the court and yelled, "All rise!"

As the door at the back opened, Judge Suzan Jenkins came out and sat in her seat.

"This court will come to order. Bailiff, can we have the first case?"

The bailiff approached the judge with the case file. She glanced at the file, then looked up at the court and said, "Prosecutor, you may present your case."

Brett stood up from his chair and said, "Thank you, Judge. I would like to ask Mr. Dustin Samuel James, to the witness stand."

I turned as Dustin slid from the pew and walked down the aisle to the witness stand, placed his right hand over the Bible, then sat in the seat on the witness stand.

Brett Matthews approached the witness stand first.

"Hello, Dustin. How long have you known Samantha Bennett?"

"About ten years, sir."

"Uh-huh, and in that amount of time have you ever seen Mr. Charles Bennett?"

"Well, when we were kids he was never around, but in the past five years or so Samantha and I have been jumped by him and his followers."

"What do you mean by 'jumped'?"

"Well, one time Samantha and I were going down to the neighbors' house, and on our way, two of the followers, I'm not exactly sure who, came up behind me and knocked me out. When I came to, Samantha was gone."

"I see. Thank you, Your Honor."

Brett turned and sat back down while the other attorney approached the stand and began asking questions.

"Dustin, you said that you couldn't see who jumped you. How do you know it was one of Mr. Bennett's followers and not someone else? Maybe Samantha just went to get help."

"Because when I came back to the house, Samantha wasn't there. The next day she came up lying on Guardian, one of our horses. I ran over to her and her clothes we torn and stained with blood. I carried her to the truck and rushed her to the emergency room."

The attorney smiled and said, "Thank you, Dustin. I would like to call Charles Bennett next to the witness stand."

Dustin got dismissed from the witness stand, and my father approached it.

"Hello, Charles. How long were you married?"

"Seven years; it would be seventeen years now, except she passed away twelve years ago."

"I'm sorry for your loss. How did you balance losing a wife, and becoming a father and mother on top of work?"

"It wasn't easy, but I tried my best, loving Samantha the best way I knew how."

"Thank you, Charles."

He turned and sat back down while Brett got up and went to the witness stand.

"Mr. Bennett, you said you loved Samantha the best way you knew how. Can you specify that for me?"

"Like you do other children, you know—hugs, kisses, tucking them in after a bedtime story, taking them out for ice cream...."

"OK. Describe a typical day when Samantha lived with you."

"I would get up early and make breakfast, go wake her up for school, and then we would have breakfast together before I drove her to school. Then I would pick her up form school around three in the afternoon. I would drop her off at home, and then I would have to go back to work until around five. Once I got home I would make dinner, and then we would play a board game and have story time."

"Really, are you sure?"

"Yes, why do you think I would lie?"

"I don't know, are you?"

"No."

"So, you have no idea what these photos and videos here are?"

Brett walked over to the table and picked up my worn book bag I'd held onto since I was ten years old, and dumped the contents onto the table. He motioned for a TV to be brought into the courtroom, then he began to hold up pictures.

"These pictures in my hand are of your 'daughter,' which she took of herself, dating back to when she was around seven years old."

I remembered taking the pictures through the mirror as I would see my reflection. Seeing the scars from belts, human contact, hangers, tree branches, and a whip, along with the mixed colors of the bruises all over my body brought flashbacks of the pain and agony. I wanted to run out of the room and go curl up and cry, but I knew for myself I needed to face this one more time in order to put it all behind me. A few minutes later, the TV was set up and ready to roll. Brett picked up the last video, which was dated July 17, 2018 at 5:18 a.m.

"This video is the last video journal of Samantha's life at Charles Bennett's house. Watch and see. I must warn you, it is very heart-wrenching and graphic."

He walked over to the TV, placed the video in the VCR, and pressed play. The video began with me in the kitchen making something—probably breakfast, considering the time. I was in some worn blue plaid bottoms and a gray tank top that were both too big for me, considering how horrifically skinny I was. My hair looked like it hadn't been washed for days and you could faintly see the bruises on my arms and shoulders under the kitchen lights. A few minutes passed on the video, and around 6:00 a.m. I began rushing, and kept glancing at the clock.

When the table was set for four with everything laid out and served, I stood waiting by the kitchen sink as my father and the three men came and sat down. My father took one glance at the food, then at me; then he took a sip of the coffee, spat it out and started to cuss and yell.

"You worthless worm, this coffee tastes terrible! Are you trying to poison me, the person who takes care of you and provides shelter and food for you? I work my tail off at work, and this is how you repay me? You're a no-good disgrace!"

He jumped out of his chair and it fell to the floor. Then he lunged at me, grabbing my shoulders, and shook me vigorously and violently right before he threw me across the floor and into the kitchen wall. He stomped over to me as I lay helpless on the floor and began kicking me with such force in his work boots I swear you could hear ribs cracking through the speakers.

Brett turned off the TV and turned to the jury.

"Jury of the court, just imagine living every day of your life like that, with this happening multiple times a day for years on end. That video you just watched actually began fairly well compared to all the others. Think about that."

He sat down in his chair, and the other attorney got up onto his feet and said, "Judge, I would like to call Miss Samantha Bennett to the witness stand."

I glanced from Brett to the attorney, to the judge, and back at Brett, astounded. Brett nodded at me, so I got up and walked to the witness stand. The attorney approached me slowly, with determination burning in his eyes.

"So, Samantha, how old are you?"

"Twenty."

"Right, and how old were you in that video?"

"Well, in that video I was twelve years and two months old."

"How do we know that these videos and photos are not of someone else?"

"Well, I can go into each tiny little detail on each picture and video if you wish, but that would take hours, if not days, which I'm sure we don't have—nor would the jury want to do, if I am not mistaken."

"No, I'm sure we don't. But what about your mother? I noticed that she wasn't in any of those photos or that video."

"Well, she wasn't in that video because she had passed away before then. See, my father murdered her on my sixth birthday. We were setting the table, my mother and I, and my mother was talking to me in Indian, as she was part Cherokee. I remember my father coming in all mad and yelling at my mom. Then as we sat down at the table, he pulled out the gun and fired it at her. She collapsed onto the table, her eyes open but hollow, staring right at me, with her mouth oozing out blood onto the table-cloth. I remember screaming. When I ran towards my mother my father yelled, 'Samantha, go to your room—and if you ever speak of this to anyone, I will personally kill you myself!' I bolted up the stairs and ran into my room and cried myself to sleep. If you don't believe me, check for a tape dated May 13, 2012."

The attorney turned and faced Brett asking, "May I see the tape dated May 13, 2012?"

Brett looked through the set of tapes to find the appropriate tape and handed it to the attorney. He walked across the room to the TV and played the video. Sure enough, my word became reality for everyone in the courtroom. The room stood in silence as if someone had just received devastating news. An uncomfortable, eerie feeling overwhelmed the room. The attorney stopped the tape, took it out, and turned to me, only to walk back to his seat. It was like he wanted to protest that the tape was false, but he just couldn't. The sadness and sorrow in his eyes said it all.

Judge Suzan Jenkins spoke after a pause. "Thank you Samantha, you may sit down."

I sat back down in the chair next to Brett. I didn't realize how nervous I had gotten until I sat back down to find my whole body shaking.

"If there are no more witnesses then I will reside a recess, and we will report back in three hours at 2:30 p.m. to hear the jury's verdict. Dismissed!"

Everyone left for lunch and the agonizing wait began. Dustin tried to make me eat the sandwich we ordered across the courthouse, but I was too anxious and nervous. I couldn't imagine my stomach handling food at the moment. After what felt like a lifetime of waiting, it was finally time to go back into the courthouse to hear the verdict from the jury. We all sat in our seat and waited. Shortly after, one of the jurymen stood up and said,

"On November 15, 2026, we find the defendants, Mr. Charles Wade Bennett, Mr. Ray Kenneth Parker, Mr. Joe Henry Johnson, and Mr. Fred Matthew Williams, guilty."

Chaos erupted throughout the courtroom. People screamed a mix of "Boo!" and "Hurray!" And if that wasn't bad enough, Mr. Charles Bennett bolted from behind the table running and screaming at me, "You filthy brat, you are going to pay for that!" My heart began to race and my body stiffened; without thinking I started to back up towards the wall, fear written across my face.

The bailiff ran at Mr. Bennett with the help of three other guards and wrestled him to the ground, bringing him back up in a secure arm lock. The judge banged the mallet and yelled over the crowd, "*Order, order, order!*" Once the room calmed down, the judge spoke.

"Mr. Bennett, I will not tolerate that kind of attitude in my courtroom. Now, finding you and Mr. Ray Kenneth Parker, Mr. Joe Henry Johnson, and Mr. Fred Matthew Williams guilty, I place you all under life-long sentences. Dismissed!"

My eyes lit up and an overpowering feeling of relief overcame me. I looked up to the ceiling with my hands up high and spun around. When I took my eyes off the ceiling and back onto the courtroom I saw my father for the last time, thrashing, trying to escape the guards' grasps, glaring at me with menacing, evil eyes. I didn't care, for as of that minute I was free and safe at last.

April 26, 2027 at 8:25 a.m.

Dear God,

Today I am writing to You in my diary a thank-you letter. Thank you for saving my life and showing me what a true Father looks and acts like. I've been through quite a lot in my twenty years of life, but if I hadn't been put through those situations I would've never found You the same way I did; or maybe not at all.

Thank you for placing Dustin and his parents in my life as my guardian angels here on earth as a way to show me that not all men or families are like mine was. They are such a blessing in my life and, between You and me, I really pray and hope that I will marry Dustin someday. We have been through so much together, I can't imagine being with someone else for the rest of my life.

The words "thank you" don't really seem good enough words to, well, thank You for all You've done and continue to do in my life; but I know to You the words "thank you" are more than enough. It's just such a blessing to be a part of Your family and not have to change or prove myself to You. For You accepted me into Your family, even though I failed You in so many ways and sometimes still do. I am one of Your many children whom You love and care for, no matter the details of our past. For Your Son, Jesus Christ, died on the cross for our sins; therefore, no matter what our pasts may contain, You still brought me and others to the cross. A Father's fatherly love, full of grace and mercy; what more could a child ask for?

I love You always.

Samantha Bennett

Chapter 10

CHANCE AT NEW BEGINNINGS

I have set you an example that you should do as I have done for you. I tell you the truth, no servant is greater than his master, nor is a messenger greater than the one who sent him. Now that you know these things, you will be blessed if you do them.

—John 13:15–17

IT HAS BEEN six months since my father, Charles Bennett's, arrest and court trial.

Dustin decided to join Skyler, Adam, and Layn on a hunting trip up in Jackson, Wyoming for the weekend.

"Babe, are you sure you're going to be OK here, on the ranch, by yourself?" Dustin asked me in a worried tone.

"Yes, Dustin, I will be just fine. I put all of the emergency numbers on the fridge and in my cell phone. Besides, I have Yeller and Ranger here to protect me."

Even with the reassurance of the numbers and the dogs, Dustin still had a worried look on his face.

"Dustin, now go have fun with the boys and you can tell me all about it when you get back, OK?"

I went over and gave Dustin a heartfelt hug. As I did so, I gazed into his big, soft, dark brown eyes. Dustin smiled that boyish-handsome smile of his and leaned in to give me a soft, tender kiss on the lips.

"Dude! Book a hotel for the night or hurry it up, or we will lose a day of hunting!" Skyler shouted from the truck.

Dustin and I both looked at him then at each other and busted out laughing.

"Well, Sam, looks like I'd better get in the truck before Skyler actually makes a reservation at a hotel or something," he said with a sigh and a grin.

"OK," I said with a sarcastic laugh.

Dustin climbed into the truck and they drove off and onward to Wyoming.

"Man, Dustin, how long have you been going out with Samantha?" Skyler asked.

"Aside from knowing her since we were kids, almost three years. Why?"

"I don't know, I thought you would have proposed or something by now...."

"Wow, that sure was forward of you to say, Skyler!"

"Sorry Dustin, I just thought..."

"Why, were you going to take Samantha from under me for yourself?"

"Well..."

"Wait! Do you have a crush on my fiancé?"

Adam put on the brakes and quickly pulled over, and all went silent. Adam, Layn, and Skyler turned to face Dustin, eyes wide and mouths gaping in shock.

"When did you decide this, and when were you planning on telling us, Dustin?" Adam asked with surprise.

"A year ago—and this weekend."

"A year? Wow, that's a long time to be thinking, Dustin. Why?" Skyler asked suspiciously.

"Well, I wanted to wait for the right moment. With all Sam's been through, I wanted to wait for the time in her life when she would be able to enjoy life without worry or fear."

"Dustin, I don't think Sam has ever felt fear or worry when she was with you. Actually, she looks at peace and secure when you're around her...like all troubles have left her world for that moment or somethin'," Layn said.

"Layn I didn't know you were such a deep, sensitive guy," Skyler laughed.

"Aw, Skyler you're just jealous that you never had the brains or common sense to act like a gentleman. And yet you wonder why women don't like you!" Adam yelled.

Skyler's face turned as red as a pack of strawberry Twizzlers. His sea-blue eyes widened; looking into them would remind you of looking into the deep ocean; and his mouth parted as if he had something to say, but not a single word escaped his mouth. Adam turned back around, brought the engine back to life with a turn of the key, and pulled back onto the road.

"Congrats, Dustin, I'm happy for you and Sam," Adam said.

"Yeah, me too," Layn commented.

"Yea, Dustin, congratulations," Skyler muttered.

"Thanks guys, that means a lot."

Adam, Layn, Skyler, and Dustin came back from the hunting trip late Sunday evening.

When I saw them through the kitchen window, driving down the windy dirt road, I set down the dishes and bolted for the door. I ran as fast as my legs would allow me towards the truck, screaming Dustin's name at the top of my lungs. Once Adam had put the truck into park and they had gotten out of the car, I lunged myself into Dustin's arms. I lifted my head and rested my chin on his firm chest, gazing into his rich, chocolate-brown eyes. A sigh escaped my lips, followed by a smile of pure love and compassion for this man I love. Dustin laughed a soft, quiet laugh and smiled that boyish smile of his, then leaned in to lay a tender kiss on my forehead. He stepped back, staring at me as if he were admiring a valuable work of art. He ran his rough, strong hand through my hair and looked deep into my sea-blue eyes.

"I love you, Samantha Elizabeth Bennett."

"I love you too, Dustin Samuel James."

We both smiled and Dustin wrapped his arm around me as we walked towards the house hand in hand.

May 25, 2027 at 6:15 p.m.

Dear Diary,

This weekend alone was so nice, but weird at the same time. Having the house and ranch to myself for the most part, except for when Dustin's parents were home, was very strange and lonely sometimes.

I took Guardian and Debonair both for a ride around the ranch and to Heaven's Peak, where we watched the sunset every night. With every sunset, the next day was even closer, therefore, I was closer to seeing Dustin.

When I saw the boys coming up the driveway, I was so excited! I was so happy that Dustin was finally home! I can't wait to hear about how his hunting trip went and all that they caught.

Samantha Bennett

Chapter 11

TODAY, TOMORROW, AND FOREVER

Many waters cannot quench love; rivers cannot wash it away.

—SONGS OF SOLOMON 8:7

TODAY I WOKE to the smells and sounds of freshly brewed coffee, sizzlin' bacon, and warm pancakes. I couldn't help wondering, what was the occasion and who would be making breakfast at four o'clock in the morning? So, I got out of bed, ignoring the calls from my bed to come back to sleep, and went downstairs to get answers to my questions. However, halfway down the stairs I stopped, for there was a rope across the stairs that said:

Your escort will be with you momentarily.

I sat on the steps flabbergasted and waited...fifteen minutes passed, and then I heard the clanging of spurs on boots and Dustin came through the archway to the dining room. He was dressed in a tucked-in, red and blue plaid button-up shirt, worn dark blue jeans, the first-place belt buckle from the national horse judging competition in Kentucky, where we first met, his dressy cowboy boots and spurs, and his battered black hat with a turkey feather in the band from his hunting trip a few weeks ago. My mouth gaped in awe as I observed him head to foot and back again, and stopped at his face. I wondered, why is he all dressed up, and why didn't I change out of my nightgown?

"Well, hello, ma'am. Come right this way."

Dustin removed the rope and held out his hand towards me. I hesitated for a second wondering what was going on, but in turn I gave him my hand, and he escorted me towards the back patio. He came to a standstill once we went through the screen door. My heart skipped a beat as my eyes saw a little picnic set up under the maple tree in the distance. I turned my head to look up at Dustin and say something, but before a single sound could escape my mouth, he put his finger to his lips, then to mine. Dustin led me to the picnic, where we sat and began to enjoy the best breakfast ever made.

"Hey, Dustin..."

"Babe, don't ask, just enjoy."

We ate in silence 'til neither of us could eat any more. Dustin got up and went behind the maple tree and came back with my riding clothes.

"What's going on Dustin?" I asked questioningly.

"You'll see. Now, go put these on and come right back."

Dustin handed me my clothes and I ran back towards the house to get changed. My mind was swimming with questions. What was going on, and what was Dustin hiding? I bolted back out the door to the maple tree, and when I came to a halt, Dustin was standing a few yards away holding Guardian and Debonair on either side of him. I ran down and greeted him with a big hug and a priceless smile. He laughed and smiled back as he handed me Guardian.

"Let's go for a ride, shall we?"

"Oh, yes, lets!"

Dustin and I both jumped into the saddles of Guardian and Debonair and headed off towards the back of the property. We stopped at the top of Heaven's Peak under the oak tree overlooking the river, trees, and rolling hills below. Both of us dismounted the horses and stood in awe of the spectacular view as the sun began to rise. Dustin turned to me, taking my hands, and knelt before me, saying...

"Like 1 Corinthians 13:7–8 says, my love will always protect, always will be trusted, always have hope, and always be preserved for you. My love will never fail as long as we are together. Will you be my wife today, tomorrow, and forever?"

Dustin took a box from his pocket and opened it. A glistening ring appeared before my eyes as he awaited an answer. My eyes began to water as I looked from the ring to Dustin...

"Yes, Dustin, I do!"

EPILOGUE

May 19, 2029 at 8:18 a.m.

Dear Diary,

You are looking at the new Mrs. Samantha Elizabeth James! That's right, Dustin and I are officially married, as of thirteen hours and eighteen minutes ago! Can you believe it? I can. The wedding was a dream come true! We had it at The James Family Ranch on Heaven's Peak. It was perfect! I had a strapless, long, elegant white dress and my hair was half pinned to the side. The bridesmaids' dresses were strapless and a light shade of orange with jewels down the side of the dress that shimmered in the sunset. You hear people say the bride will walk down the aisle; well, as I saw Dustin waiting for me under the wedding arch, which was decorated in orange and white flowers with golden leaves glistening in the light with Layn, Adam, and Skyler beside him, everything around me vanished. All I could see was him standing there with his manly, boyish smile all dressed up in his pretty tux, looking right at me. I felt like I couldn't breathe, like this was a dream, but I kept walking down the aisle, with Yeller slowly but surely carrying the rings in front of me, dressed in a little doggie tux. It was very cute and funny, if I do say so myself. We said our "I do's" and of course kissed for like the umpteenth time, except this time it was a deeper, more sincere, and passionate kiss that lasts a lifetime.

Dustin and I left the altar as Mr. and Mrs. Dustin Samuel James, a little white carriage wrapped in orange and gold ribbons with Guardian and Debonair driving us into the sunset and onward to Scotland at the sounds of their hooves...the sounds of a Happily Ever After....

Samantha Elizabeth James

—∿∿—

Twelve years of a great marriage have flown by, with more greatness to be experienced. The honeymoon to Scotland was an amazing trip full of grace, love, and compassion that grow stronger every day, like seeing a fairytale unravel its story before my husband's and my eyes. No matter if we were on foot, on horseback, or just admiring the view, we were—and still are—very blessed.

As a wedding present from Dustin's parents we became the sixth generation of Jameses to live on the ranch.

"Sam, baby, time for breakfast. Adam, Layn and Skyler are joining us and will be here around eight thirty."

"What time is it?"

"It's eight."

"OK, I'll get the kids and be right down."

"Babe, I already got the kids up. Nora is helping

Luke clean up the playroom, and Canaan is in his
room asleep. I came to wake you before I went to
wake Canaan."

"Well, seeing as you are on top of things, I guess
me and baby-on-the way will see you at the dining
table."

I headed downstairs while Dustin went to wake
Canaan for breakfast. As I turned the corner I heard
little feet running.

"Mommy, Mommy, Mommy!" Luke and Nora
yelled.

"We got the play room all cleaned up!" Luke and
Nora said with excitement.

I laughed and smiled as they wrapped their little
arms around my waist and legs and gazed up at me
with big, curious eyes.

"Did you, now? Well, y'all are big kids to be helping
Mommy and Daddy."

I knelt in the middle of them, my arms open
wide for a big bear hug. They laughed and giggled
as their arms embraced my body.

"Let's go eat."

We headed to the dining room hand in hand.
Dustin came down with little Canaan in his arm.
Luke and Nora sat in their chairs while Dustin set
Canaan in his high chair by me. Right after Dustin
had put the last of the food and drinks on the table,
we heard a truck pull up and the doors shut.

"Oh, I bet that's Adam, Layn, and Skyler."

"Uncle Adam, Uncle Layn, Uncle Skyler!" Luke and
Nora cheered as they jumped from their chairs and
toward them, arms open wide.

"Hey, how's my little man Luke?" Skyler asked as he picked Luke up into his arms.

Luke smiled and replied, "I'm good. Guess what, Uncle Skyler?"

"What?" Skyler asked curiously.

"I helped clean the playroom! Come see!"

Skyler laughed as he said, "You're becoming the man of the house, are you now? Show me."

Skyler set Luke on the floor and followed him as he ran towards the playroom.

"How's my little princess Nora?" Layn asked her as he picked her up.

"Good."

Everyone went back to the table and had a fulfilling breakfast with one another. After Luke and Nora finished their breakfast, they went to play in the playroom. Layn, Skyler, and Adam cleaned up the table. I carried Canaan to the living room and met Dustin on the couch. Shortly after, Adam, Layn, and Skyler joined us in the living room.

"Man I swear those kids get bigger every time I see them. How old are they now?" Layn asked.

"Well, Luke is eight, Nora is six, and Canaan here is two," Dustin replied as he reached to take Canaan.

"I don't see how y'all do it with another one on the way. When are you due, Sam? Do you know if it's a boy or girl?" Skyler asked.

I laughed a soft laugh and replied, "I'm due in about two months on April tenth, and "it" will be a boy. Enough about us, what have you guys have been up to?"

Layn replied first, "Well, still doing rodeo, mainly bull riding though. So I'm on the road pretty much all the time. I'm leaving for San Antonio, Texas next weekend."

"Wow, never thought you would leave Skyler without someone to do team roping with."

"Yeah, you'd think, but I did because he's been spending all his time with a 'Miss Someone'."

"What? Skyler, really? You've finally moved on from Sam? Ha-ha," Dustin said in a loud, laughing voice.

"Yes, surprising, I know. I met her at the rodeo dance in Oklahoma six months ago."

"Wow, congrats. I'm surprised she's been sticking around considering your past experiences with women."

"Ha-ha, yeah sometimes I wonder that too. I'm a very lucky man if I do say so myself."

"Yep. How about you, Adam? How's Emily? Any new additions to the family?"

"Emily and I are great; I can't believe we've been married eight years already. Bo will be turning five tomorrow and Noah will be turning three this September. Emily and I are going to surprise Bo with a black lab puppy tomorrow for his birthday. So, the puppy will be the newest addition to the family for now."

"Aw, it's amazing how fast the kids grow up. Seems like just yesterday we were bringing them home from the hospital," I commented.

"I agree, they grow up so fast," Adam said.

Before long it was time for Layn, Adam, and Skyler to leave. Dustin led them to the door with Canaan, while I went to get Nora and Luke from the toy room to say goodbye. We all gave hugs and kisses to one another and the boys were off. Luke and Nora chased after their truck down the road for a few yards, waving goodbye while Canaan, in Dustin's arms, Dustin, and I waved from the porch.

Another glorious day on the James family farm, and many more to come, full of love and happiness.

ABOUT THE AUTHOR

Hello Reader,

I am Laurel Payne, the author. I grew up in Texas during my childhood until God took the next chapter of my life to Kansas. I have grown up with a love of horses; naturally, being from Texas. I have ridden horses my whole life, both Western and English with a little of polocrosse. I competed in the Red River Region Pony Club for about ten years. As I look back on it now, and still to this day, I see that God used and uses horses as an outlet for me and as a way to show me what it means to have a loving, caring, and trusting relationship with someone and know that they will love, care, and trust me back.

When God came into my life in December of 2007, He told me, "It's OK, Laurel. You are safe now. I got you." My life changed from not knowing what love really was or what it meant to be loved, to knowing what love is and what it means to be loved. God led me to Kansas State University, where He has shown me what it means to have a true family that loves and cares for me. Though my past and present life has not always been "easy," God has always been there; even if I did not always know or realize it. Without God in my life I would not be here. I love Him with such heartfelt passion! I cannot wait to see where He takes me in the next chapter of my life....

CONTACT THE AUTHOR

http://toyoufromgod.weebly.com/